PRAISE FOR
SHARYN McCRUMB'S

SICK OF SHADOWS

"A fine and often humorous novel, a
whodunit with multiple motives and rich
characters."

Los Angeles Times

"This witty mystery is a book to read twice.
First for the story, then for a chuckle at
McCrumb's dry humorous style, which must
be savored slowly."

Lexington Herald-Leader

"A delightful, spooky romp among the mad
and wise of a southern family. A grand
debut."

—Dorothy Salisbury Davis,
Author of *Tales for a Stormy Night*

"Quite terrific! I couldn't resist it!"

—Otto Penzler, Publisher
The Armchair Detective

"Lively... hilarious... Sharyn McCrumb
offers up some zany characters, clever dialogue and an ingratiating heroine... lots of
fun."

Alfred Hitchcock Magazine

"... all mystery fans have a treasure in
Sharyn McCrumb. If Evelyn Waugh had writ-
ten mystery stories set in the American
South, he might have produced *Sick of
Shadows*."

—Fred Chappell,
Author of *I am One of You Forever*

Other Avon Books by
Sharyn McCrumb

SICK OF SHADOWS

Coming Soon
HIGHLAND LADDIE GONE

Avon Books are available at special quantity discounts for bulk purchases for sales promotions, premiums, fund raising or educational use. Special books, or book excerpts, can also be created to fit specific needs.

For details write or telephone the office of the Director of Special Markets, Avon Books, Dept. FP, 1790 Broadway, New York, New York 10019, 212-399-1357. *IN CANADA:* Director of Special Sales, Avon Books of Canada, Suite 210, 2061 McCowan Rd., Scarborough, Ontario M1S3Y6, 416-293-9404.

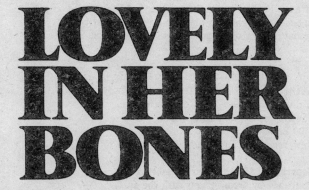

LOVELY IN HER BONES

SHARYN McCRUMB

AVON
PUBLISHERS OF BARD, CAMELOT, DISCUS AND FLARE BOOKS

LOVELY IN HER BONES is an original publication
of Avon Books. This work has never before appeared
in book form. This work is a novel. Any similarity to
actual persons or events is purely coincidental.

AVON BOOKS
A division of
The Hearst Corporation
1790 Broadway
New York, New York 10019

Copyright © 1985 by Sharyn McCrumb
Published by arrangement with the author
Library of Congress Catalog Card Number: 84-
091626
ISBN: 0-380-89592-7

All rights reserved, which includes the right to
reproduce this book or portions thereof in any
form whatsoever except as provided by the U.S.
Copyright Law. For information address Hintz
Literary Agency, 2879 North Grant Boulevard,
Milwaukee, Wisconsin 53210.

First Avon Printing, July 1985

AVON TRADEMARK REG. U.S. PAT. OFF. AND IN OTHER
COUNTRIES, MARCA REGISTRADA, HECHO EN U.S.A.

Printed in the U.S.A.

WFH 10 9 8 7 6 5 4 3 2 1

AUTHOR'S NOTE

Although this is a work of fiction, about an imaginary Indian tribe, I have tried to be as faithful as I could to the reality of Appalachia and to the science of forensic anthropology. I would like to thank the scholars who helped me in my research, and to absolve them of any blame for liberties I have taken with the information provided. Thanks to Dr. David Glassman, for graciously allowing me to audit his forensic anthropology course at Virginia Tech; Dr. David Oxley, Roanoke medical examiner; Officer Mike Meredith, Virginia Tech police department; Dr. Jean Haskell Speer, Appalachian Studies Program; and to the following naturalists for help with plant lore: Clyde Kessler, Janet Rock Alton, Elizabeth L. Roberts, and Clarence "Catfish" Gray.

The Cullowhees are based on several groups of "racial isolates" in Appalachia and elsewhere, and their social and political situation is consistent with the actual experiences of some of these groups.

To my father,
        for my roots in Appalachia

I knew a woman, lovely in her bones ...
—Theodore Roethke

LOVELY
IN HER BONES

CHAPTER ONE

"I KNOW it's my turn to cook," Bill MacPherson informed his roommate. "I'll fry a chicken on one condition."

"What's that?" asked Milo, absently collecting his scattered papers from the kitchen table.

"You have to promise *not* to tell me which leg of the chicken I'm eating. And I'm not interested in its age or gender either!"

"Sorry," grinned Milo. "Reflex action. You show me a bone and I analyze it automatically. Did you know I can approximate the height of the bird from a drumstick?"

"Well, don't! It's a bad habit. People don't want to get that intimately acquainted with their dinners. I know you live and breathe forensic anthropology, but you don't have to think about it constantly. Do I talk about law all the time?"

"Okay, man. I promise. No autopsy on the fried chicken. I'll go study in the living room."

"All right," grumbled Bill. "You've got about an hour."

Milo padded off to the living room with an armful of notes and a human-origins text, which he proceeded to spread out on the coffee table in front of the window. Bill shook his head and began to cut up the chicken. Milo was a little overzealous in his archaeological studies, but he was a decent guy. He didn't let mold grow on his laundry like the last roommate, and he wasn't a selfish swine like the one before that, who used to bring girls home unannounced at midnight and had expected Bill to go off and sleep in the law library. Bill had laid down the law about that the day Milo came to look at the apartment, and Milo had replied cheerfully: "Don't worry! If I bring home any girls, they'll be dead!"

It turned out that he was a research assistant to Dr. Lerche, the university's forensic anthropologist. Milo acted as lab instructor for Dr. Lerche's classes in archaeology and human origins and assisted him on cases for the state medical examiner. Lerche and Milo were called out to find bone fragments after house fires or to identify bodies too far gone for recognition or fingerprints. To Bill's great relief, Milo didn't bring any of his casework home, but he did haul in a few lab specimens from time to time, to reattach a mandible to a fragile skull or to prepare some samples for the undergrads to study.

Bill had grown so used to Milo's bizarre form of clutter that he hardly noticed it any more, but Milo's habit of treating fried chicken as a lab exercise still grated on his nerves. He put the wet chicken into a plastic bag containing flour and assorted spices (old family recipe) and shook vigorously. Now what came after that? He peered at the recipe card propped against the saltshaker. He had remembered to dip the pieces in butter and egg this time. His family still laughed about his first attempt at frying chicken, when he'd had to call long-distance for instructions, making it one of the most expensive home-cooked meals he'd ever prepared. Well, he could hardly be expected to clutter his mind with recipes, considering all the trivia he was expected to memorize in law school. Another couple of months of it and he'd be reduced to writing his phone number on his hand for lack of brain space.

"Now here's an interesting specimen!" yelled Milo from the living room.

"Oh, really?" called Bill politely as he dipped a drumstick in hot oil. He decided to humor the zealot. "How so?"

"Bipedal, orthognathous ... pyramidal-shaped mastoid process ... foramen magnum facing directly down ..."

"Neanderthal?" guessed Bill, mispronouncing the word.

"No. Your sister. She's coming up the walk."

Bill came to the kitchen doorway and saw that Milo was looking out the front window instead of at his anthropology notes. Elizabeth was coming up the walkway toward the building. "I suppose she'll want to be fed," he grumbled, doing a quick mental tally of chicken pieces.

"I hope she doesn't want to cook!" said Milo. "She's got her herb bag with her."

"I'll be firm," Bill assured him. "I'm not drinking any more of that concoction of weeds that she calls tea."

"What was it last time? Fennel and rosehips?" Milo shuddered. "Does she really know what she's doing? She's only been in that wretched course for three weeks."

Bill shrugged. "I taped the rescue squad number to the side of the phone."

"Well," sighed Milo, "if she poisons us, give me to Dr. Lerche for the lab."

The doorbell rang.

Bill's younger sister, Elizabeth, who had just graduated from the university in June, had—after a brief adventure at a family wedding—returned to the university to take summer courses while she tried to decide what to do with her degree in sociology. ("What's it gonna be, Elizabeth? Burger King or grad school?" Bill would say.) She was presently enrolled in an Appalachian studies course in folk medicine, and she was developing an alarming tendency to try out her brews on Bill and his roommates.

"You're just in time for dinner," Milo was saying as he ushered her in the door. "But I warn you right

15

now: if you make us drink any of your herbal swill, I intend to do an autopsy on the chicken."

Elizabeth made a face at him. "It isn't swill!" she retorted. "Herbal tea contains no caffeine, no additives, and aids in digestion. In Scotland they—"

Milo took a deep breath. "The epiphysis of the avian femur—"

"But I didn't come here to make tea!" she continued loudly, drowning him out.

"Safe!" muttered Bill from the kitchen.

"I came to consult you," she said to Milo with frosty dignity. "Would you follow me to the kitchen, please?"

Milo obediently trailed after her into the kitchen, where Bill was turning over pieces of chicken in the iron skillet. "Go ahead," he told her. "I'm listening."

"Well, it's really Milo that I wanted to talk to."

Bill shrugged. "Be my guest."

"Okay." She hoisted her blue canvas bag onto the table and leaned against the back of a kitchen chair. "Our assignment for tomorrow was to find three woodland herbs, and since I didn't want to get the same stuff everybody else was finding, I took the car and drove a few miles out of town to look around in the woods out there."

Milo groaned. "Okay. What did you find? Some fraternity's marijuana crop?"

"Poison oak?" snickered Bill. "Or—not kudzu! I refuse to taste kudzu in any form!"

Elizabeth wrinkled her nose. "I don't think kudzu is edible," she decided. "But I can ask tomorrow in class if you want me to."

"No, that's okay," said Milo quickly. "Just show me what you found."

"This!" said Elizabeth dramatically.

She unzipped the canvas bag and set the skull in the middle of the kitchen table. In the center of its forehead was a neat round hole.

16

CHAPTER TWO

ELIZABETH noted their astonished faces with satisfaction. She folded her arms and waited. "Well?"

"I'll phone the police," Bill said hoarsely.

"No! Wait! Let me take a look at it." Milo shook his head. "In the first place, Elizabeth, you shouldn't have moved it. The police want to see a gravesite as undisturbed as possible."

"Well, I didn't want to just leave it there!" Elizabeth protested.

"Yeah, that's a natural reaction," Milo conceded. "I suppose you'd be able to find the place again? Did you mark it or anything?"

"No, but I think I could find it."

Milo looked as if he wanted to embark on a lecture, but he checked himself, merely remarking: "Oh, well, as long as it's here I might as well take a look." He picked up the skull with practiced familiarity and peered at it closely. The lower jaw was missing, and many of the upper teeth had been broken out. The brain case was discolored with brownish streaks, and the back of the head was a gaping hole of jagged perimeters, parallel to the neat round hole in the forehead. After a moment's scrutiny, Milo said simply, "It's real."

"Of course it's real!" said Elizabeth indignantly. "What did you think it was? Plastic?"

Milo shook his head. "No. I know it's a human skull, but I thought it might have been part of a skeleton swiped from a med school or doctor's office. That's been known to happen. I just checked for little steel pins in the skull, which would have held the mandible in place. They aren't there, so it's no lab specimen."

"Well, of course it isn't!" snapped Elizabeth. "I told you I found it in the woods! It's a murder victim. Don't you see that bullet hole in the forehead?"

Milo smiled. "Sure, I see it," he told her. "People bring skulls like this to Dr. Lerche every now and then. Usually they turn out to be lab specimens or skulls from an Indian grave. And about twice a year, we get Yorick brought in."

"Yorick?" echoed Bill.

"Yeah. You know—the skull from the drama department. Some fraternity wise guys steal him every so often and leave him on the steps of a girls' dorm or on top of a parking meter. Then somebody finds him and brings him to us, thinking they've discovered Jimmy Hoffa or something."

"But—this isn't Yorick?" asked Elizabeth, pointing to the skull.

"Oh, no," Milo assured her. "I know Yorick on sight. This guy is much younger. And he's been in the ground awhile. Yorick is bleached a nice glossy white."

"Anyway, Yorick didn't have a hole in his forehead, did he?" asked Bill.

"Not the last time I saw him," said Milo. "But that's what I started to tell you. We get skulls brought in with bullet holes in them, but they're usually not murder victims. They're skulls from Indian graves or people who died from natural causes, and some hunter has found the skull and used it for target practice."

Elizabeth sat down. "Oh," she said in a small voice. "I never thought of that."

"Sure. It's amazing what clowns some people are. So before we jump to any conclusions about murder, we examine the bullet hole to see if we can determine whether it's a new hole in an old skull or the original

18

death wound." He lifted the skull again and peered at the small, neat hole.

Bill and Elizabeth watched the examination in uncomfortable silence. Finally Elizabeth burst out: "Stop being so mysterious, Milo! Tell us what you think!"

Milo looked thoughtful. "Well, I wouldn't want to say for sure without Dr. Lerche to back me up, but if you insist on having an answer right this minute . . ." He glanced at his audience and saw that this was indeed the case. "Okay, now remember I can't be positive, but I'd say that the indications are that this is not a postmortem injury. There are no cracks radiating from the entry wound, and the bone on the inside of the hole is the same brownish color as the exterior. New breaks show whiter bone."

"You mean he was murdered?" asked Elizabeth, leaning down to look at the skull.

"I think he was shot while he was still alive," said Milo carefully.

"Same thing!" Elizabeth declared, slapping the table. "Hah! I knew it! Call the police, Bill."

"Hold it, Bill," said Milo. "I'd like to check out the site before you get the cops out there tramping all over the evidence. This guy"—he pointed to the skull—"has been in the ground for at least five years, judging by those soil stains and root marks. Another couple of hours isn't going to make much difference."

"Five years, huh?" said Bill thoughtfully. "Did anybody disappear around here five years ago? Wasn't there a camper from Richmond . . ."

Milo gave him a disgusted look. "You don't think it's that easy, do you? It could be five years or fifty, Bill. Once it's been in the ground for more than two years, it's hard to pinpoint age. I mean, I can tell you that this guy died around age . . . oh . . . twenty-five to forty . . ." He ran his fingers along the lines on the top of the skull and nodded. "Yep. Say thirty-five

19

when he died. But I don't know whether he was thirty-five in 1980 or 1880. It's a tricky business."

"A lot of help you are," Elizabeth remarked.

Milo stood up. "Well, I might do better if I could see the actual site. Take me to where you found him."

Bill flipped off the burner under the pan of chicken. "I take it nobody's hungry any more?"

No one paid him any mind. Elizabeth got up and was following Milo into the living room, listening to him expound on the fine points of site investigation.

Bill gazed sadly at the skull, still sitting in the middle of the table. "I don't suppose you're hungry either?" He tossed the potholder on the countertop and went off to join the expedition.

"Why do I have to sit in the back? My legs don't bend this way!"

"I'm driving," said Elizabeth, glancing at her brother in the rearview mirror. He was stuffed into the back of her Volkswagen, all legs and elbows, looking like an improperly folded jack-in-the-box.

"I'm consulting," said Milo. "Consultants always get the front seat. You're just a tourist. Now, Elizabeth, how far is this place?"

"Couple of miles. Don't worry. I know where I'm going. It's on your side of the road, past a church, a couple of barns, and a darling little black goat."

"A darling little black goat!" mimicked Bill. "Gimme a break! Whatever possessed you to take this screwball course anyway? Couldn't you find one on Scottish history?"

Elizabeth frowned. "They don't offer one here. Anyway, I don't see why you tease me about being interested in the family origins. If you aren't proud of being a MacPherson, I certainly am."

"Well, if you're interested in the family origins, you ought to take Milo's course," Bill suggested.

Elizabeth glanced at Milo. "Oh? What are you teaching?"

"Uh . . ." Milo looked uncomfortable. "I'm just the lab instructor, really."

"For anthropology? I knew that. Are you doing a course on Scotland?"

"No. On the evolution of man. You know, cavemen, evolution . . ."

Elizabeth directed a glare at the rearview mirror. "I'm not interested in tracing the family as far back as that, thank you!" she snapped.

"Well, I wish you'd consider it." Bill grinned. "Anything would be better than having you stewing weeds every other night."

"Why did you pick that course?" asked Milo quickly to forestall the sibling argument in the offing.

Elizabeth thought for a moment. "I probably got the idea from my Uncle Robert."

"Dr. Chandler?"

"Yes. He's been writing a book on colonial medicine for as long as I can remember. It's practically all he talks about. When I visited him, he mentioned the different herbs the pioneers used to use as medicine—like ginseng. He said that scientists today are just beginning to realize that some of them really worked. I thought it was an interesting subject, and since this course was being offered, I decided to take it. And it does *not* involve stewing weeds!" she finished loudly for Bill's benefit.

"Well, it certainly—"

"Excuse me," said Milo loudly. "Is that the goat?"

Elizabeth slowed down to get a better look at a calf-sized black billy goat nibbling bushes in a pasture beside the highway. "That's him," she announced. "The road I took will be the next one on the left. It'll be blacktop for about half a mile, and then it turns to gravel."

"Wonderful," groaned Bill. "A nice secluded area to go searching for bodies."

"If you're afraid, you can wait in the car," said Elizabeth sweetly.

To the people who lived thereabouts, the road probably had a name, but to the Virginia Highway Department it was only a three-digit number, one of thousands of back lanes, too insignificant to appear on anything besides a county map. It began at the main road, dividing unmown pastures whose barbed wire ended at red clay ditches on either side of it. One meandering driveway led off to a farmstead before the blacktop gave way to dusty gravel, at which point the road began to parallel a rocky creek whose banks formed a steep grade on the right side. Beech and oak trees arched their branches over the road until they touched, forming a green awning patched with sunlight. On a bright July afternoon the effect should have been that of a peaceful country scene; any feelings of foreboding must have been in the minds of the beholders.

Bill scowled at the trees darkening the road. "What did you expect to find down here? Hemlock and wolfbane?"

"Don't you like it?" asked Elizabeth. "I think it's rather pretty. Except that it seems a little more deserted than I noticed the first time."

Milo sighed wearily. "You guys won't be happy until you see a sign welcoming you to the "Twilight Zone," will you? Really, you're making too big a deal over this."

"Oh, sure," said Bill. "What's one more skull, more or less? You're used to it."

"Okay. Okay." Milo held up a restraining hand. "Just don't get out your cloaks and daggers until I look at the site, okay? If it turns out to be a murder, you two can go back and—I dunno—arrest the goat!"

"Our consultant is a comedian," said Elizabeth sourly. She pulled off the road and parked the car in a flat space between two trees. "This is where I stopped last time. I left the car here and walked up the bank there through the trees."

Milo opened the door. "Okay," he told her. "Retrace your steps and we'll follow. Let's try to keep single file if we can, so we don't trample any more of the site than we have to."

"Do you want me to get the tire iron out of the trunk?" asked Bill.

"Suit yourself," shrugged Milo, "but don't expect to use it. Whoever did this—*if* anybody did it—has been long gone. Those earth stains on the skull didn't get there overnight."

"There wasn't anybody around," said Elizabeth. "I didn't see a house or any other signs of human habitation. It's just—woods."

"Then how did *he* get here?" muttered Bill.

"Well," said Milo, "I was going to say 'Your guess is as good as mine,' but it probably isn't. Ask me again after I've seen where she found him. Lead the way, Elizabeth."

For several minutes they walked in silence up the slope of a wooded hill, threading their way around underbrush and fallen tree limbs. Elizabeth had to be dissuaded from stopping once at an outgrowth of ferns and once when she wanted to investigate a prickly-looking plant she thought might be burdock. Bill and Milo vetoed any botanical detours and urged her onward.

"What else can you tell about this guy?" Bill asked Milo.

"Judging from the size of the bones and the nasal cavity, I'd say the skull is that of a male Caucasian," Milo answered. "I could be more sure in the lab, where I could make precise measurements and compare the data to the discriminate function chart."

"What's that?" asked Bill.

"Joe-pye weed, I think," said Elizabeth. "Can I pick some?"

23

"No!" snapped Bill. "And I wasn't talking to you. You keep walking. You're not lost, are you?"

"Of course not!"

"I was asking Milo about some chart or other he mentioned."

"The discriminate function chart," said Milo. "It's a set of statistics on skull measurements for blacks and Caucasians. When you have to identify a skull, you measure certain points—nose width, angle of the jaw—and compare your findings with the standards on the chart. That ought to give you a pretty good idea whether the person was male or female, black or white."

"What if it's a big woman or a very small man?" asked Bill.

"Well, I didn't say it was foolproof. It's dealing with averages, after all. But Dr. Lerche says he'd rate it at ninety percent accuracy."

Elizabeth came to a stop and looked around. The slope had leveled off to a small clearing that extended for about twenty feet to the base of a steep hill, which rose above their heads like a cliff. The clearing itself was ringed by oak and pine, and carpeted with grass and pine needles instead of underbrush.

"This is the place," said Elizabeth softly.

Milo studied the landscape. "Uh-huh," he nodded. "I bet it is."

"Why did you say that?" Bill demanded. "Have you been here?"

"No," said Milo. "It's just a hunch. Look, why don't you two look around in the clearing here for more evidence, and I'll go walking around a bit farther off. Maybe to the top of that ridge there." He nodded toward the steep embankment in front of them.

"You're not going too far, are you?" asked Elizabeth nervously.

"No. I'll be within earshot. If you find anything, give a yell. Look for bits of cloth on bushes or other bone fragments in the dirt. They may be pretty hard to spot, so be careful where you step."

"And what will you be looking for?" asked Bill.

"Oh, same kind of thing," said Milo, smiling. "Whatever I can find. I'll be back in ten or fifteen minutes."

"Where should we start?" asked Elizabeth.

Milo considered the question. "Start where you found the skull and gradually branch out in a circular pattern," he advised her. "I'll see you in a little while."

He strolled over to the foot of the steep hill and inspected it, as if he were looking for the most solid pathway to the top. After prodding at a few small rocks, he headed off into the trees, where the ridge began to slope at a gentler angle. Bill and Elizabeth knelt in the pine straw and began to sift through it in search of bone fragments. First, Bill patted the ground with his open hands to see if he felt any bonelike projections, and Elizabeth scraped away the leaves to get a better look at the soil itself.

"Milo really knows his stuff, doesn't he?" she remarked.

"He ought to," said Bill sardonically, thinking of drumsticks.

"It's pretty interesting, too. It must be neat to look at a heap of old bones and be able to tell all about the person they belonged to."

"Ummm. Here's something! No, sorry. Just a rock. Are you sure this is where you found it, Elizabeth?"

"I keep telling you: yes."

"Well, I don't see any other bones. Maybe the murderer dropped it here and scattered the rest of the bones all over the county."

Elizabeth looked up. "That's a thought," she said, digesting the idea. She pictured a hulking figure with a motorcycle propped against a pine tree, fishing bones out of a black leather saddlebag. "Why don't I go over to the trees and work toward you? We'll cover the whole clearing faster that way."

"Good idea." Bill nodded.

"Just be sure you look very carefully. Some bones are pretty small."

Twenty minutes later they had managed to work back together, having covered most of the clearing with nothing to show for their efforts except jeans streaked with clay from knee to ankle. Elizabeth pushed her hair away from her face with a sweaty forearm. "Whew! This isn't as easy as I thought it was going to be," she said. "Maybe we should start looking for the murderer's tracks."

Bill groaned. "Milo said five *years*, Elizabeth. Use your head!"

"Oh, that's right. I forgot."

"I wish we'd brought some beer. It's hot out here."

"Well, I wouldn't mind getting hot and dirty if we'd found something," said Elizabeth.

"Hello down there!" called Milo from the top of the ridge. "Made any great discoveries?"

"Get down here!" Bill yelled back.

Milo grinned and made a mock bow. He skittered down the steep side of the embankment, arms outstretched, shifting his footing from one small rock to another. In less than a minute he had made a final bound into the clearing and stood beside them brushing off imaginary dirt. He looked disgustingly clean and eager.

"No rusting and bloody chainsaw?" Milo asked them, beaming. "No buried Viking longboat?"

"Shut up and tell us what you found," Bill demanded.

Milo became serious. "I think we can call the authorities now," he said solemnly. "This man was murdered."

Elizabeth shivered. "I knew it!" she said softly.

"And I can describe the murderer," Milo concluded.

They stared at him. "How?" they said in unison.

Milo held up a hand for silence. He began to pace as though lecturing a class. "The killer in this case was a white male, between the ages of twenty and forty-five, probably from New York or Pennsylvania, and he was wearing a dark blue suit at the time the killing took place." He nodded at his audience, gaping at him from a kneeling position.

"Milo, that's incredible!" Bill burst out. "Did you get all that from a site investigation?"

Milo grinned. "In a way," he chuckled. "It says on this guy's tombstone that he was killed at Antietam, so the rest was easy to figure out."

Elizabeth jumped up. "Are you telling us that this guy was killed in the *Civil War?*"

"Right."

"I thought you said five years," Bill reminded him.

"I also said that after something has been in the ground, age becomes very difficult to determine," said Milo.

"But he wasn't in the ground," said Elizabeth. "He was just sitting there in the middle of the clearing. And there *wasn't* any tombstone!"

Milo smiled. "Yes, there was," he said, pointing to the steep hill in front of them. "It's up there. There's a little family cemetery on the top of that hill, and this guy was buried on the edge near the embankment. After so many years, the coffin rotted, the hill eroded some, and *voilà!* The colonel rolls down the hill."

"So there was no murder," said Bill, "and all this was for nothing."

"Oh, I don't know," Milo replied. "I was serious about informing the authorities. I'm sure the family will be glad to have Great-Grandpa, or whoever he is to them, restored to his proper place in the family plot."

They began to walk back down the wooded slope toward the car.

"Now can I stop and look at plants?" asked Elizabeth.

"No," snapped Bill. "I'm hot and tired, and we haven't had supper."

"But I only have two plants! We were supposed to bring in three."

"Tell them about the skull," Milo suggested. "They can't argue with that."

"It is pretty interesting." Elizabeth agreed. "Even if it wasn't a murder case, it was fascinating to see what you could tell just from looking at bones."

"Oh, I'm no great shakes at it," said Milo. "You should see Dr. Lerche in action."

"How did you get to be his assistant anyway?" Elizabeth wanted to know.

Milo grinned. "It's a long story. I'll fill you in on the way home."

Milo refused to tell his story until the car windows had been rolled part of the way up so that he wouldn't have to shout above the wind, then he waited until the car had turned off the gravel road and back onto the main highway.

"There's the goat, Milo," said Elizabeth. "You can start now."

"How did I get to be Dr. Lerche's assistant?" Milo asked thoughtfully. "Well, it was because of something that happened when he first came here to the university. I was an undergrad in anthropology in those days, and I worked as a security guard in my dorm—sort of like a night watchman. I handled the small stuff and turned the rest over to the campus cops. The hours were murder, though, since I had to get up and go to class the next day, and I wanted a lab job in the department. I had bugged everybody else in the department without success, so when Dr. Lerche arrived with his new Ph.D. to set up a forensic anthro lab, naturally I went to him straight off and asked if he needed any help."

"And he hired you?" asked Elizabeth.

"No. He said he'd let me know. He didn't even have his lab set up at that point; most of the equipment hadn't even been ordered."

"So when did he hire you?"

"The next day. Now shut up and let me tell you how it happened." Milo leaned back against the seat and tucked his hands behind his head. "Okay. Dr. Lerche had already met the district medical examiner because the two of them would be working together on cases. You know forensic anthropologists consult for the state, right?"

They nodded.

"Well, that same day I talked to him, they had a case come in. It was a found body in a pretty bad state of decomposition, and—"

"Wait a minute," Elizabeth interrupted. "Is this story going to get gross?"

Milo thought about it. "Not really," he told her. "I won't get any more graphic than I have to."

"Okay," said Elizabeth grudgingly. "Go ahead."

"All right, the medical examiner brought Dr. Lerche this body and wanted a report on it right away. That meant that he had to get down to the bones quickly so he could go to work." He glanced over at Elizabeth to see if his explanation had been delicate enough.

"Don't pay any attention to her," said Bill. "Go ahead. How did he do that?"

"Well, the method he uses is to boil the body until the flesh comes off—"

"Aargh!" Elizabeth made a face.

"But he didn't have any place to do it. See, his equipment hadn't arrived, and he didn't want to do it in his apartment—"

"Thank God!" said Bill, grateful that precedent had been established.

"All right," sighed Elizabeth. "What did he do?"

"He called the animal science people and asked if they had any facilities that he could use over in their building."

"That seems reasonable," said Elizabeth cautiously. She had been dreading a mention of the cafeteria or some other bizarre site.

"Sure, it was," Milo agreed. "They offered him their lab facilities right away. The only problem was that the only thing they had for boiling things in was an autoclave."

"That thing you sterilize instruments in?"

"Yeah. And you know how small it is. No way you could get a whole body in one of those things."

Elizabeth sighed. "I know I'm going to hate myself for asking this, but—"

"Well, he just put it into the autoclave a piece at a time, right, Milo?" asked Bill.

"Of course. What else could he do? The process was going to take at least twelve hours to do anyway. He started at six o'clock, as soon as the animal science people had gone home for the day. And he just stayed there that night, tending his autoclave and stacking up the clean bones."

"What does this have to do with you?" asked Elizabeth.

Milo grinned. "There he is, by himself, dressed in ragged cutoffs and an old T-shirt because it's ... uh ... inelegant work," he finished lamely with a glance at Elizabeth. She nodded solemnly, and he continued. "It's three o'clock in the morning, not another soul in the building, when suddenly the door to the lab bursts open and in walk three campus cops, guns drawn."

He waited for a moment so that Bill and Elizabeth could grasp the situation. Elizabeth nodded slowly, "So—*they* think—"

"Oh, sure! They think they've caught Jack the Ripper's grandson! And he doesn't have any identification on him. It's in his good clothes, which he left in his office. At three o'clock in the morning, who's he going to call? Remember he'd just gotten here and didn't know many people."

"Did they arrest him?" asked Bill.

"Yep. He tried to explain what was going on, and they allowed him to go without handcuffs on the strength of that, but they were going to take him down and put him in a cell until they got things straightened out."

"He went to jail?"

"No." said Milo. "That's where I come in. Three a.m. was my break time, when I walked across campus to Burger World for something to eat. That's what would keep me awake until breakfast time. So I'm strolling past the animal science building when the three cops come hustling out the front door, clustered around a prisoner. I knew the cops, of course. They'd stop in and pass the time with me every now and then. I said hello to Boyce and Wade, and then I saw who it was they'd arrested. Dr. Lerche and I recognized each other at the same time, in fact, but before I could say anything, Dr. Lerche said: 'This man can identify me! He is my new lab assistant.' "

"So you identified him?" asked Elizabeth.

"Oh, sure. I would've anyway, but when he said I had the lab job, I would've let him be whoever he wanted. The cops apologized and left, and Dr. Lerche and I went over to Burger World and drank coffee and talked. I've been working for him ever since. It's a great job."

"It sounds interesting," Elizabeth agreed. "I'd like to study bones—what do you call it?"

"Forensic anthropology. Would you like to work on a dig some time? We often use students as field workers, and I could probably get you hired. I know Dr. Lerche isn't teaching second summer session, so he might be planning to do field work somewhere. Are you interested?"

"It sounds wonderful," said Bill.

Milo turned to gape at him. "You mean *you'd* like to come along?"

"No. I was thinking of getting rid of the two of you for the rest of the summer. Six weeks without bones or weeds. Wonderful!"

CHAPTER THREE

ALEX didn't know she was there. His office door was open, but she had heard him in conference with a student, so she waited in the hall without announcing her presence. She didn't mind waiting. It would give her time to decide what to say.

Tessa Lerche studied the bulletin board beside the door of her husband's office. It contained the usual end-of-term notices posted by undergrads: ride needed to D.C. area; apartment to sublet; textbooks for sale—cheap! Nothing ever changed except the phone numbers. The "Professional Typing—Reasonable Rates" looked like the cards she used to post when Alex was in grad school, the lean years when a few term-paper jobs meant the difference between peanut butter and hamburger. At the time those years had seemed a long prologue to what she had thought of as "real life." Looking back now, she saw that time as a golden age. Alex had studied a great deal, but he had also talked to her about his work. She had typed his papers. Now his work was put on computers by one of his assistants, and he seldom discussed it. Perhaps she should have continued to go on digs with him as she had out west, but over the years her interest had decreased and she had been less willing to spend blazing summers in the desert. She was thirty-three now. Her looks wouldn't stand the weeks of roughing it as they used to. Once you passed thirty, you couldn't take your looks for granted. She jogged, and moisturized her skin regularly, and she watched her diet. Sometimes people still mistook her for an undergrad. Alex never seemed to notice, though. He came home for dinner; there was no nonsense about worrying where he was or with whom, but even when he was at home . . . he wasn't. He'd eat his dinner in an abstracted way, making polite murmurs to her attempts at conversation, and he'd spend the rest of the evening at his desk in the den, hunched over a column of figures, while she read or watched television. When she asked him what was the matter, he'd shrug and say, "Nothing," or that he was tired, or the work wasn't going well. She had decided that their marriage was in a seven-year slump, a thing to be waited out as gracefully as possible—until this morning's discovery had convinced her otherwise. She had been straightening up Alex's desk—which he preferred her not to do—when she found the yellow legal pad he made notes on. Scribbled in the margins beside data on Paleo-Indian cultures were the words "Mary Clare" written over and over.

"Excuse me, ma'am. Are you waiting to see the professor?"

Tessa looked up, wondering what her expression had been. The man was not a student. He was tanned and wiry, nearing forty, with a head so bald that he must have shaved it. He had the sort of brown eyes that can express feelings, and at the moment his were radiating concern for this distraught stranger he'd found in the hallway. He might be one of Alex's colleagues, Tessa realized. Whoever he was, he was waiting to see Alex, and he would be listening outside while she said whatever she was going to say to her husband.

"You feeling all right?" he asked gently.

She forced herself to meet the man's eyes. "I—I got an F," Tessa stammered, and fled.

Alex Lerche blinked at the visitor who sat on the other side of his desk toying with a Sioux buffalo-jaw

34

knife. People usually commented on the fur and beadwork on the hilt, but the bald man in the khaki jumpsuit was running his fingers along the iron blade with an expression of cheerful inquiry.

"Wouldn't be a bad hunting knife, but I'd hate to have to take it into combat."

"Combat?" Lerche considered it. "I don't think the Sioux—"

The visitor smiled. "I was talking about Nam. Spent a couple of years there in Special Forces. I was acquainted with a couple of Indians over there, and nary a one of us carried one of these."

"You're interested in Indians, Mr. . . . er . . ."

"Comfrey Stecoah. Reckon I am interested in Indians, seeing as how I am one. I'm looking for Dr. Lurch. Might you be him?"

"It's pronounced Lair-ka," the professor murmured. The correction was automatic. "It's a Danish name. And you say *you're* an Indian?"

"Uh-huh," he grinned, reading the thought on Lerche's face. He did not look like most people's conception of an Indian, and he knew it. He was tanned, but not as dark as many of the Southwestern Indians; his features included a nose too broad to fit the stereotype, and—since he was shaved bald—his hair was a matter for speculation. "I came to see you because I hear you're an expert on Indian cultures."

"I have done some work with Plains Indian cultures," said Lerche cautiously. "What would you like to know?"

"It's not a question of knowing. It's a question of proving. I know your work involved the Indians out west, but you're the closest thing we got to an expert in these parts, so you'll have to do."

Lerche smiled in spite of himself. "What, exactly, will I have to do?"

"My people want you to conduct an archaeological expedition on our land. Well, that is, it *should* be our land—to help us win our case."

Lerche sighed. "Could you start at the beginning before I get any more confused?"

Stecoah grinned. "Sure. It's like I said, my people—"

"Stop right there! Now, start with that. Who are your people?"

"The Cullowhees. We're an Eastern Indian tribe up in the Appalachian Mountains. It's a couple of hours' drive from here. You ever heard tell of us?"

Lerche hesitated. "I've heard of the Cherokees," he offered.

Stecoah sighed. "Who hasn't? Well, we're not them and they don't need your help. They got their craft shop and their outdoor drama, and—oh, hell, who am I to knock that? I wish we had a deal like that."

"The—Cullowhees, did you say?"

"Yeah, we're a right small group. Less than a thousand folks, all living in the same little valley. But we don't have any tribal recognition from the U.S. government, and we don't have any tribal land. That's where you come in. We need some help from an outside expert to help us get a land grant from old Uncle Sam."

Lerche tapped his fingertips together as he considered the matter. "I guess it could be done," he said finally. "If you get me some tapes of your tribal language and some samples of your pottery and other artifacts, and we could—"

"We can't do it that way. We need you to do some digging to find evidence that this was our land. There's a cemetery in the valley where our people have been buried for at least a hundred and twenty years that we know of. That ought to count for something with the government, shouldn't it?"

"I suppose so, but wouldn't it be simpler to get someone to do a study of your cultural patterns and link you up with the Cherokee or the Iroquois, so that you can get tribal status by association?"

"Wouldn't work."

"I seem to remember it being done that way once."

"Yeah, but it wouldn't work for us. We don't do pots, ner tomahawks, ner any of that craft stuff. Never have. And the only tribal language we got is the one I'm a-talking right now."

Lerche digested the information. He had no experience with Eastern Indians, but his work in the Southwest had led him to expect some vestiges of original culture, regardless of the years of exposure to white customs. How could they have lost all of it and still keep together as a tribe? It had the makings of an interesting study.

"Do you know anything about your origins?"

Stecoah leaned forward and put the knife back on the desk. "Now personally, I don't hold much with the origin stories," he drawled. "I reckon it's enough that we're Native Americans without having to put on some kind of dog-and-pony show about where we came from. But I know that if we're goin' to run this one by the Department of the Interior, that's the kind of damnfool thing people are going to be asking."

"I would imagine so," Lerche agreed. He was listening to the man's rounded vowel sounds, hoping for some sort of distinctive accent, but to Lerche's unpracticed ear, Stecoah sounded just like the few Appalachian people he had met.

"The trouble is can't nobody agree on where we came from. Some people want to think we're descended from the Indians and settlers of the Lost Colony, but I don't believe it. That was all the way across North Carolina on the coast. We're mountain people. My mother claims we're descended from a tribe called the Unakas who intermarried with some Moravian missionaries from Salem. Then there's folk who claim some of Daniel Boone's people left the party around the Cumberland Gap, and that they moved in with the local tribe, and that we're the descendants of that mixture. It don't matter a hill of beans to me, as long as we get the land. Which story do you reckon they'll like the best in Washington?"

"I really couldn't say," murmured Lerche. "Perhaps I could recommend a qualified anthropologist who could study the matter for a few years and produce some kind of a theory based on more evidence."

The door swung open and Milo, shrugging off his white lab coat, shouldered his way into the room. "Hey, Alex, I don't know what—" He looked up and noticed the visitor. "Sorry. I didn't know you were in conference."

Alex smiled. "Milo, Mr. Stecoah is a representative of the ... ah ... Cullowhee Indians."

Milo looked impressed. "Pleased to meet you, Chief."

"Thanks. I'm not a chief. We don't go in for that stuff. I was a master sergeant in the Army, though."

"Mr. Stecoah wanted to consult us about a dig on his people's land. He needs some authentication so that his group can apply for tribal status with the government, but I was telling him—"

"You been stonewalling me," Stecoah growled. "Talkin' about some kind of fancy study taking a couple of years. We don't have that kind of time. The government's about to turn our land over to some damned coal company for strip mining! We need help in a hurry, or we'll have us a Trail of Tears, just like the Cherokees." He grinned. "I'd rather have an outdoor drama like their'n, if it's all the same to you."

Alex Lerche hesitated. He was as ecology-minded as the next person, but he was uneasy about committing himself to such a project on short notice. He sighed. "Perhaps we could discuss this a bit further," he offered. "Milo, do you have time to sit in?"

"Sure. Class is over. This sounds like a great idea

38

to me!" He caught Lerche's warning glance and subsided into polite interest.

"It might be a good idea for you to make some notes as we go along," Lerche told him.

Milo tilted his chair back toward the door and reached in his lab coat for his pen. "Oh! I almost forgot what I came in here for," he said, withdrawing a piece of paper from the pocket. "I found this in the hall and recognized your handwriting."

Lerche took the piece of paper with the words "Mary Clare" scribbled all over the margins. It was the data sheet he'd left at home on his desk with the notes for his journal article. "Where—"

"I bet that lady dropped it," said Stecoah. "She was waiting to see you, but she looked mighty upset."

Alex stared at the sheet of paper and let the calamity sink in.

He knew that Tessa had found the paper. That was the only way it could have appeared in the hall outside his office. The fact that she had brought it must mean that she had decided to have a confrontation. He wondered if she would believe the truth, and even more if he could bring himself to admit it. He would have to talk to Tessa, though, before she did anything drastic. Women, he thought ruefully. At the skeletal level, the only difference between women and men was a piece of bone the size of his hand, but—he smiled to himself—the antemortem differences were vast. Tessa was going to be difficult about this, just when he needed all his energy to work on the discriminate function chart. That was what was really important. Couldn't she see that? He wished he could just get away.

Silence. Lerche became aware that the two people whose existence he had forgotten were staring at him expectantly.

"Er—what?" he asked uneasily.

"The dig!" Milo prompted him. "What do you think? It would give you more data for the chart."

"Not to mention helping out some *live* folks," Stecoah grunted.

Alex blinked at them. "Yes, all right. We'll go."

Mary Clare Gitlin, graduate teaching assistant in anthropology, had discovered that she could grade multiple-choice tests to the beat of almost any song played on the local country radio station. "It wasn't God" (mark one wrong) "who made honk-" (mark one wrong) "y-tonk angels" (no mistake). She didn't care whether this was a coincidence or a revelation of some major truth about human behavior. It relieved the monotony of grading a hundred freshman quizzes. The rest of the graduate assistantship was proving most enjoyable, she thought. Alex Lerche was certainly a nice man to work with. She was lucky she hadn't been assigned to Dr. Ziffel, an irritable pedant nearing retirement after a mediocre career, who resented every talented student in the department. The few times she had encountered him, he had made a point of imitating her East Tennessee accent, his derision masked as a social smile.

Alex was a little too serious, but she preferred that to Ziffel's bitter humor. Alex was dedicated. He had a trick of leaning forward when he talked to you, and of using his hands with the fluid grace of a mime, painting his meaning with an economy of perfect gestures. To Mary Clare's way of thinking, he looked like a scientist, while the rest of the department looked like a bunch of bureaucrats. They went to class in suits and ties and pretended their first names were Doctor, but Alex seemed oblivious to the trappings of academia. He showed up for class in corduroy jeans and a white shirt rolled up to the elbows, with his white blond hair combed in a wave across his forehead. Every now and then he'd come in wearing a suit jacket and tie—and you knew that *she'd* picked out his clothes that morning—but by ten o'clock he'd look the same as always and be engrossed in the puzzle of an old bone, like a happy bloodhound. Mary Clare smiled to herself. He was a nice man and a good scientist. It seemed a waste to have him cooped up in a classroom teaching general anthro when he could be doing important fieldwork. Someone with Alex's skill and knowledge should be out there making discoveries all the time, not just on occasional field trips for the undergrads' benefit. Mary Clare circled the F she had written on the top of a quiz. What a waste! Still, in fairness to Alex, she didn't think the university job had been his idea. The person who wanted a secure income, faculty prestige, and a fancy house instead of a campsite—that wasn't Alex. It was *her*. Mary Clare sighed. Best not to speculate on what doesn't concern you, but it was a pitiful shame just the same.

Tessa applied the wire whisk to the bowl of eggs with more force than necessary, making a yellow and white maelstrom in the mixing bowl. Tonight was quiche night, since this had been her afternoon for volunteer work at the Crisis Center and she had her aerobics class at seven. Alex would be home soon. From her worktable by the kitchen window she could see the driveway, and she found herself watching for the car with increasing apprehension. It was not dread so much as a last trace of stage fright before the beginning of a performance.

She had talked about it that afternoon with Ginny at the Crisis Center, and they had decided that she was overreacting. A name on a piece of paper was hardly evidence of adultery, Ginny had pointed out, but she conceded that the situation would bear watching. The important thing was to remain calm and keep the lines of communication open. She told Tessa to remember that although the male libido was an emotional form of pond scum, men did not really want to leave their wives. Infatuations were simply passages in ego gratification; infantile, of course, but

41

what else could you expect? She advised Tessa to behave just as usual, only more loving, more attentive, and more understanding. Finally she had given her a photocopied article on "Advanced Degrees as Community Property" and enrolled her in the center's divorce law seminar. It never hurt to be prepared.

Tessa was sliding the quiche pan into the oven when she heard the car door slam, ending an imagined series of conversations between her and Alex. ("Of course you're not having an affair with her, dear. You wrote her name on your notes because you have discovered the missing link and are thinking of naming it after her!") Should she walk to the front door to meet him, or would that seem too artificial? What should she say?

She decided to stay where she was for the sake of the psychological advantage (the kitchen was her sphere; besides, she had to get supper out of the way in order to be on time for her class). When Alex came in, she was setting the table.

"Dinner's nearly ready," she told him. "I have to rush off to my class, but if you'll leave the dishes on the countertop, I'll do them when I get back."

"I always do the dishes on your class night."

"It's all right. I don't mind doing them later. Want some coffee?" *I sound manic*, she thought. *I sound like a stewardess. Trying to act normal is the most unnatural behavior of all.*

"Coffee would be fine," said Alex warily. "If it isn't any trouble."

"Not at all." Tessa began measuring coffee for the percolator. "And how was your day?"

"Oh, fine. Got an interesting case today."

"Alex—" Tessa started to say that she didn't like to hear about his gruesome cases before dinner, but remembering Ginny's advice, she amended this to: "That's nice. Tell me all about it."

"I don't know much about it yet," Alex admitted.

"A group of Indians up in the mountains wants me to do an exploratory dig to help them get tribal recognition from the government."

"Maybe I'll have tea. I've been drinking that awful instant stuff all day at the Crisis Center, and I can already feel the caffeine on my nerves."

"Tea will be fine, then, Tessa."

"No. You have coffee. I've already started the percolator."

"Whatever. Uh, anyway, this tribe wants me to find some evidence that the land they're on is traditional tribal land. Apparently there's some question of their losing it to a strip-mining operation."

"I think I'll fix a salad to go with the quiche. Would you rather have leaf lettuce or spinach?"

"Whatever's easier. I think it should be an interesting dig. I don't have any data on Eastern Indians for my discriminate function chart, and this will give me a chance to get some."

"Spinach, then. Leaf lettuce isn't really good unless you fry bacon to go with it, and there's enough cholesterol in the eggs as it is."

"It shouldn't take more than a couple of weeks. I'd be back in time for term break in case you wanted to take the beach cottage again this year."

Tessa closed the refrigerator slowly. "Back?" she echoed. "Back from where?"

"Sarvice Valley, the place is called. We'll be camping, of course, but there's a little town nearby with a tourist court, so we can rent a room there to hook up the computer in."

"You're going away on a dig?" said Tessa, comprehending at last.

"Just a minor one," said Alex faintly.

"I see." Tessa's voice was cold.

"You won't need me for anything around here, will you?"

"What makes you think I don't want to go, Alex?"

He shrugged. "Precedent."

"Well, you're right. I have too many commitments here to pick up and run to the mountains with you." Tessa frowned as another thought occurred to her. "And I suppose you'll be taking your graduate students with you?"

"Yes, of course. It will be good experience for both of them. It will be the first time for Mary Clare."

"That," said Tessa, "I find very difficult to believe."

It was well past five o'clock when Milo finished up in the lab and returned to his office. The light was still on and the door was open. Milo's office mate, Mary Clare, was curled up in her swivel chair making notes on index cards.

"Don't you ever go home?" asked Milo.

"Look who's talking," she answered without looking up.

"What are you doing? Lecture prep?"

"Yeah. Getting my facts straight. Somebody always asks me a question that requires an exact date or a statistic, and I can't quote that stuff off the top of my head."

"Neither can I, but Alex sure can. I think he's got that discriminate function chart memorized. But don't worry; I'm sure you're a good teacher."

"Good as I want to be," said Mary Clare. "I don't plan to be stuck on a campus all my life. I want to be a real anthropologist—out there doing fieldwork."

"Well, you're going to get a taste of it pretty soon. This time next week we'll be roughing it in Sarvice Valley."

Mary Clare's jaw dropped. "We're gonna be *where?*"

"Sarvice Valley. Don't you know where that is? I figured you would. Mr. Stecoah talks just like you do."

"I'll bet he does!" snorted Mary Clare, momentarily distracted. "You and Alex couldn't tell Loretta

Lynn from Scarlett O'Hara! Where's this guy from? Eastern Kentucky?"

"No. Sarvice Valley is in the area where North Carolina, Virginia and Tennessee all come together."

"That's closer than I expected," said Mary Clare grudgingly. "But y'all still don't know your accents. Now what's this about a dig? I thought we were going to be doing local work this summer while Alex finished up the discriminate function chart."

"So did I," admitted Milo. "But all of a sudden he seems anxious to go. Maybe he's just interested. The job is to authenticate an Indian tribe. Alex wants to meet with both of us in the morning, by the way. That's why I wanted to talk to you first. Since you assisted him with the field archaeology course first session, we'll probably get the diggers from that class."

"Probably. What about it?"

"I was wondering: do you think we could use one more person?"

Mary Clare sighed. "If he's moving us clear to the Tennessee line, I expect we'll need all the help we can get. A lot of my people are signed up for classes this session and won't be able to go." Her eyes narrowed. "Why?"

Milo assumed his most unconcerned expression. "Oh, a friend of mine said she'd like to go on a dig sometime, that's all."

"Oh, Lord. Why don't you take your girlfriends to dances like everybody else? Stop blushing, Milo! I didn't say no. It's all right with me, but you'll have to put up with her. I don't want any Christmas tree angels on this dig not wanting to get dirty, not wanting to get sunburned, not—"

"She'll behave." Milo grinned. "She's not the delicate type. Did I tell you she brought a skull home last week?"

"This makes the third time, Milo. Look, go ahead

and ask her to come along. Make sure she has a trowel and a sleeping bag—"

"I know, Mary Clare, I know."

"And remember, if she turns out to be a prima donna, she's your problem. I don't know why anthropologists always get tangled up with women who become millstones around their necks, like—" She caught herself and looked quickly at Milo.

"I know," said Milo quietly.

When Milo left the office, it was past six o'clock but still sunny. He cut across the upper quad, avoiding the parameters of an impromptu softball game, and took the path that led past the duck pond, sheep barns, and across the highway to Brookwood. His apartment was a fifteen-minute walk from campus, but he was in no hurry to get there. He lingered near the duck pond watching the campus waterfowl, fat from begging, glide across pools of sunlight. At the water's edge a boy in a football jersey was throwing a Frisbee over the head of a frantic Labrador retriever. Milo sat down at a concrete picnic table to think.

Because he was a comfortable-looking fellow with a kind word for everyone, people tended to confide in Milo. Perhaps they meant to compliment him with their display of trust, but his uneasiness always outweighed his gratification. "If I wanted to hear personal problems, I'd have been a psychiatrist," he told himself. "I'm a forensic anthropologist, for God's sake! I don't understand people who aren't *dead.*" He had not mentioned the paper he found in the hall to Mary Clare, because he sensed the makings of a disaster in it. He didn't even want to think about it himself. His greatest fear was that Lerche, knowing that he'd seen it, would feel obliged to give him some sort of explanation. This, Milo felt, would be very awkward for everyone. He had done his best to play dumb when he'd returned the paper; he hoped his show of innocence had convinced Lerche that he knew nothing. Mary Clare had been about to tell him something back in the office, but he had managed to forestall that, too. If this dig was going to be the backdrop for a soap opera, Milo didn't want to know the details.

Milo got up and started on the path toward the sheep barns. The sun was lower in the sky now, making the tin roofs glow red and turning the sheep into shadow pictures. He didn't want to think about Lerche's troubles any more. He wouldn't blame the man for getting involved with Mary Clare, he decided. Anybody could see that Mrs. Lerche was the Junior League type, and probably a pain in the ass as a scientist's wife, but all the same, Alex ought to be careful. Her idea of revenge might be to play the part of a woman scorned on the carpet in the dean's office. He shook his head. Maybe Mary Clare was right; maybe he was crazy to be asking Elizabeth along on the dig, but at least he'd find out what type she was before they got too involved.

Having made this resolution, Milo spent the rest of the walk home planning the fine points of inviting Elizabeth. Should he make her buy her own trowel or give her one of his old ones?

When he reached the door to the apartment, his reverie had reached the stage of imaginary dialogue in which he said bright and clever things to which Elizabeth responded with dazed admiration. He was somewhat surprised to open the door and find that she was actually there.

"Hello, Elizabeth!" he stammered. "I'm glad you're here."

"You won't be when you taste dinner," Bill warned him.

Milo sat down on the couch beside his roommate thinking about the meals he would be having for the next few weeks in Sarvice Valley. "Maybe we could send out for a pizza."

"Very funny," said Elizabeth, who had returned to the kitchen. "*Why* are you glad I'm here?"

"Well, I have some interesting news. Can you leave that stuff and come in here?"

"That's right. Distract her." Bill lunged for the telephone book. "Pizza . . . pizza."

Elizabeth adjusted the dial on the electric skillet and came back into the living room, making a dive for the phone book. Bill dodged the attack and called out Lombardi's number to Milo.

Milo picked up the phone, and then, remembering his manners, told Elizabeth: "I have a good excuse for this. I'm going to have to be eating garbage for the next couple of weeks, so I can't afford to waste any meals right now."

"Very diplomatic," Bill commented.

Elizabeth glared at him. "Do as you please." She had intended to make this her exit line, but as she turned to leave, the implication of Milo's explanation struck her. "What do you mean you'll be eating garbage for a couple of weeks?"

"Prison, I expect," said Bill. "He and Lerche are probably laundering bodies for the Mafia. I've suspected it for months."

"No, as a matter of fact, I've been captured by Indians," said Milo.

"Does this have to do with why you were glad to see me?" Elizabeth asked.

"Yes. You remember when you found the skull in the woods, and you said that you'd like to go on a dig sometime? Well, today Dr. Lerche decided that we're going on one up in the mountains, and I've arranged for you to be able to come along."

Elizabeth looked puzzled. "I don't know anything about archaeology."

"You don't have to. Only the supervisors have to be experts. You'll be one of the field crew. It's sort of like—"

"Ditch digging," suggested Bill.

"I was going to say 'gardening,'" said Milo. Elizabeth looked less than delighted, so he hurried into a more enthusiastic account of the project. He explained the Cullowhees' problem, and the general assignment: to excavate the oldest section of the burial ground to gain clues about the tribe's origin. "And besides that, Elizabeth, it will be a chance for you to be part of a team establishing new data for anthropologists. Remember the discriminate function chart I told you about?"

She nodded. "The one that enables you to tell males from females and blacks from whites? The skeletal remains, I mean," she said hastily to forestall Bill's next remark.

"That's right. The point is: there is no discriminate function chart for Indians. That's what Dr. Lerche is working on right now. It's going to be a pretty major contribution to the field. Most of the data for the chart has already been compiled from Dr. Lerche's work in the Southwest, but he's going to add the Cullowhees in to widen the sample."

"How do you mean, add them in?"

"We're excavating the old burial ground, right? Okay, when we exhume a body, we take the skull measurements, and so on, and add the data to the statistics we already have."

"It sounds very exciting, Milo, but what's the catch? I still haven't forgotten your remark about the next couple of weeks being difficult."

"That's right, Milo," said Bill. "Skip the part about grave robbing and get down to the rough stuff."

Milo, who was used to his roommate's repartee, ignored this remark. He had been about to give Elizabeth a carefully edited version of life on a dig, minimizing the discomforts and tedium, when he remembered what Mary Clare had said about anthropologists burdening themselves with unsuitable women. If he lied to Elizabeth about the rigors of fieldwork, surely he was inviting the same kind of maladjustment in the future. He wanted her to go very much, but it had to be for the right reasons. If she went merely to humor him, it might be all right this time, or even the next dozen times, but sooner or later problems would arise.

Milo sighed. "Okay, here goes. We'll be camping in the Sunday school room of a little Baptist church in Sarvice Valley, so we'll have electricity and an indoor toilet, but the showers will be rigged up outdoors, and the cooking will be strictly hot plate or campfire. And you can forget about clean sheets: we'll be in sleeping bags. We will usually work a ten-hour day, because there's not much time left in the summer to do this job, and you'll spend most of the day on your knees grubbing in hard red clay. There's no salary, and you pay your own expenses. Now, do you want to come or not?"

Elizabeth blinked. "Well, of course I want to come, Milo. I told you I wanted to learn how to read bones the way you do, besides, since you've made it sound so awful, if I don't go, certain people will never let me hear the end of it." She nodded meaningfully in Bill's direction.

"Just tell me where you want the Red Cross parcels sent," Bill remarked.

"Sarvice Valley," said Milo. "In care of Mr. Stecoah, our host."

"Stecoah?" echoed Elizabeth. "Amelanchier Stecoah?"

"No. I think this guy's name is Humphrey. No, that's not it. Comfrey, maybe."

"Comfrey! Hold on!" Elizabeth began to rummage through her tote bag from folk medicine class. She pulled out her spiral notebook and leafed through the pages, skimming her notes with her forefinger. "Comfrey is the name of a plant," she told them. "That's why I think ... ah! Here it is: 'One of the best-known Appalachian herbalists is an Indian woman, Amelanchier Stecoah, whose folk medicines and reputation as a storehouse of mountain lore have made her the subject of numerous articles and one documentary film.' Why, she's famous! And I'll bet she's one of the Cullowhees. Do you suppose I'll actually get to meet her?"

Bill, who had watched his sister's outburst with weary amusement, turned to Milo and said, "Well, I know what I'm going to do while you're gone."

"What's that?"

"Move. And leave no forwarding address."

Elizabeth laughed. "Don't be silly, Bill. What would you do without letters from me to brighten up your tedious existence? Now, I haven't got time to cook because I have to talk to Milo about the dig. Weren't you going to order a pizza?"

CHAPTER FOUR

SARVICE VALLEY, named for the white-flowered trees which covered the hillsides, had been optimistically named by its pioneer discoverers. Strictly speaking, the area was not large enough to be a valley; in local terms, it was merely a "run," which is the bottomland carved out by a small creek. The encircling mountains formed the community's boundaries, limiting its population to several dozen families farming a few acres of rocky hillside. A one-lane road turned off the main highway where tiny Sarvice Creek emptied into a stone-studded river, and it paralleled the creek up the run, turning to a dirt track long before it reached the creek's source: a trickle from a spring in a wooded hollow six miles from the mouth. At the end of the run, where it joined the main road, the hills arched up on either side of the pavement, crowding road and creek into a sliver of land. There was no room to live or farm for the first mile of the run, but after a few rises and turns the land began to level out, revealing frame houses and cornfields on either side. In the widest stretch of bottomland at the center of the run, the community had built its main street: a one-room post office and a general store. Any less basic transactions would have to be carried out in the nearest incorporated town, Laurel Cove, which was eight miles up the highway.

Although Sarvice Valley's population was 98 percent Cullowhee, there were no souvenir shops or other concessions to tourists. The area was not on

the path of the Appalachian Trail and was suffi-
ciently remote to be largely ignored by the sightse-
ers, who confined their interest to the Blue Ridge
Parkway or the Great Smoky Mountains National
Forest. Those in search of Eastern Indians found the
Cherokees conveniently situated to both, so that few
outlanders even bothered to investigate the Cullowhees. It was just as well: seekers of colorful
Indian folkways would have been disappointed by
the Cullowhees, who were indistinguishable from
their Appalachian neighbors. Those tourists who did
risk their cars' suspension systems in Sarvice Valley
were drawn there by the hand-lettered sign by the
side of the main road.

"There!" cried Elizabeth. "Did you see what that
sign said?"

"I'm not stopping at any more *Antiques* or *Scenic
Overlooks,*" said Milo.

Elizbeth pointed to the weathered board, marked
in slanting free-form lettering: AMELANCHIER—WISE
WOMAN OF THE WOODS—6 MI. An arrow pointed toward
the Sarvice Valley Road. "I told you she lived around
here," said Elizabeth.

"This is our turnoff," nodded Milo. "Be on the
lookout for a white frame church."

"I want to go and see her. She's supposed to be
over eighty, and she knows everything about root
medicine. I brought my notebook. Do you suppose
she'll take me out gathering with her?"

"Maybe. But first you've got to get moved into the
Sunday school room, do your K.P. assignment, and
go to the diggers' meeting that Alex is having after
supper. Remember, I've vouched for you on this dig.
Don't let me down."

Elizabeth was surprised at Milo's serious tone. She

had never heard him so businesslike. "I'll do my job," she said meekly.

Milo didn't answer. He seemed intent on the winding road in front of them. It lurched through oak groves and banks of mountain laurel, which parted now and then to provide a glimpse of the creek below. The only sign of human habitation was an occasional mailbox nailed to an upturned log and surounded by clumps of Queen Anne's lace and tiger lilies. Milo, oblivious to the beauty of the summer woods, wondered why he was so edgy. This was a routine excavation, after all; surely there was less at stake here than there was when he assisted the medical examiner in criminal cases. Why should he be more nervous now? He told himself that it would turn out to be two weeks on a hot, dull job. The glamour of grave robbing was vastly overrated. With an effort of will, he made himself concentrate on the routine tasks ahead.

After a few more miles of gradually broadening bottomland, the road opened up into fenced pastures, and finally to a cluster of houses comprising the community of Sarvice Valley. The church was easy to spot: it sat on a wooded hillside overlooking the village and was actually several miles farther off than it appeared.

Elizabeth looked at the weathered frame houses, whose sagging porches and battered roofs testified to their age. "It doesn't look like an Indian village," she said doubtfully.

"Very true. I think the Cherokees mostly have brick homes with carports."

Elizabeth made a face at him. "You know what I meant!"

"Something out of a John Wayne movie, I expect. The interesting thing is that with the Cullowhees, this isn't just the effects of civilization on their culture. Apparently, they've always lived and talked like everybody else. It would make an interesting study."

He drove onto a dirt side road, across a narrow wooden bridge, and steeply uphill toward the white church, which flashed in and out of their line of sight as they curved through the woods. On one side of the hill a small meadow had been cleared on the creek side of the church, for picnics and baptisms. Two cars and a van had been parked in the meadow just off the road. Milo pulled in beside the van.

"Everybody's here already, I guess. Let's get our stuff unloaded and take it up to the church."

"I thought we were excavating a cemetery. I don't see one."

"It's behind the church, but that's not the one we'll be working in. Those graves with the granite head-stones are pretty recent—1930 and on. The old bury-ing ground is farther up the hill, past a little stretch of woods."

"Have you seen it?"

"No. Dr. Lerche came up here earlier this week with Mr. Stecoah, and he did some preliminary work. He'll cover that in his lecture after dinner. Do you need any help carrying anything? No?" He slammed the trunk. "Let's go."

The Sunday school room had a plank floor, walls of unfinished boards, and a smeary copy of the *Last Supper* done on black velvet. The wooden folding chairs had been stacked by the table at one corner of the room, beside boxes of food and supplies. Five sleeping bags were laid out in the center of the room, and on one of them sat Mary Clare Gitlin playing a guitar. She had not heard them come in. Her blond hair brushed the neck of the instrument as she chorded the notes to a mountain song: "Love, oh love, oh careless love. Look what love has done to me."

"Hello, there!" said Milo, more loudly than necessary.

"Hello yourself, stranger," called out Mary Clare. "What took you so long?"

"Well, that road was no picnic. I never tried to drive over a washboard before. And then I had a passenger who wanted to stop at every tourist trap on the highway." He nodded toward Elizabeth. "Mary Clare, this is Elizabeth MacPherson. She's ... uh ... a friend of mine."

Mary Clare extended her hand to Elizabeth. "Pleased to meetcha. I haven't heard a thing about you," she said with a smile that made the statement patently untrue.

"So, who's here?" asked Milo, looking around.

"Alex, of course. He's up at the site poking around. And two guys from my intro class volunteered to come for the experience. I don't know if you've run into them or not. Victor Bassington and Jake Adair."

Milo made a face. "Bassington. Yeah. He hangs around the department all the time. Know-it-all. But you mean that's it? Six of us?"

"Six of us staying here. We got four more people coming in for daytime, but they'll be going home at night. Alex got them from the state archaeological society."

"Amateurs?"

"Seems like it. College undergrads, at best."

"What about consultants?"

"None at the moment. The Carolina guy is off at a conference, and the folks at U.T. have a big project of their own going. Maybe one of them will check our stuff later on. Nobody's an expert on Cullowhees, anyhow. They're such a small group, and so lacking in distinctive cultural features, that nobody ever got around to doin' 'em.' "

Milo smiled. Mary Clare's accent was still a mixture of East Tennessee dialect and sociologist's jargon. Four years of college hadn't made much of a dent in it, he was glad to see. As an anthropologist he was all for people maintaining their cultural heritage. Too bad the Cullowhees had lost theirs; things would have been much easier if there had been a few clues to go on. Maybe something would turn up at the gravesite.

"Well, anyway, I'm glad you're here. Milo, why don't you hunt up Jake and Victor and get the van unloaded while Elizabeth helps me set up Alex's slide projector?"

Milo looked stricken. "What about supper?"

Mary Clare smiled mischievously. "Why, Milo, it's real sweet of you to offer, but it isn't necessary. Mr. Stecoah has arranged a covered-dish supper here at the church so that the Cullowhees can meet us. They're even going to sit in on Alex's introductory lecture."

"Won't that be dull for them?"

"I don't know. Alex seems pretty excited." Her eyes shone. "I think it's going to do him a world of good to be away from that old college."

Milo looked uneasy. "Yeah ... well ... I guess I'd better start unloading the van. See you later, Elizabeth."

"I guess he's rather tired," said Elizabeth quickly. "It was a long drive up here. Why don't you show me what you want me to do?"

Two hours later, the Sunday school room had been transformed into a dining hall by the addition of two dozen folding chairs and three card tables covered with sheets. The residents of Sarvice Valley had arrived in small groups, carrying bowls of beans and potato salad, meatloaf, pans of cornbread, and homemade cakes. They had eyed the diggers shyly at first, talking among themselves, but finally one stout woman had marched up to Elizabeth and Mary Clare and asked: "Which one of you'uns is married to that professor?"

"Neither one of us," said Mary Clare just as bluntly. "We're hired on. His wife stayed home in a big old brick house."

The woman nodded, satisfied. The answer seemed to fit her idea of the way the world should be run. "You ain't married atall?" she asked. Why, they must be twenty-one if they was a day, she reckoned.

"Not yet," said Elizabeth, trying to soften the blow.

"Reckon somebody ought to plant you a love vine."

"What's that?" asked Elizabeth, sensing an item of plant lore.

"It's a flower grows up in the hills. That's what we allus calls it. Love vine. You plant it and name it after your sweetheart, and if it lives, why, he'll take a shine to you."

"Are you Amelanchier?" asked Elizabeth in a hushed voice.

The woman laughed. "Shoot far, no! Why, Amelanchier wouldn't eat two smidgeons of what's on them tables. She's up home, most likely, or out a-gathering. It don't take her know-how to plant a little old love vine. I could do it easy. Who would you want me to name it after?"

"Alexander," said Mary Clare softly.

Elizabeth opened her mouth to say "Milo" when he suddenly appeared at her elbow. She hastily amended her answer to "Robert Redford."

"Alexander and Robert," nodded the woman happily. "That ought to do the trick." She hurried back toward the dessert table.

"Hi," said Milo. "How's it going?"

"It's interesting," Elizabeth answered cautiously. "I don't think I've met everyone yet."

"They're still sizing us up," Milo told her. "Don't you find their accents interesting?"

"What accents?" asked Mary Clare.

He laughed. "Anyway, you ought to meet the rest of the team. This is Jake Adair," he said, nodding toward a dark-haired young man in jeans who was chatting with a pudgy fellow in gray slacks and a blazer. "That's Victor Bassington he's talking to. Come and meet them."

Because of Jake's flashing smile set off by a deep tan, Elizabeth decided that he must be Spanish or Italian. He set his plate down and shook hands with her. After a disinterested hello, Victor wandered off to refill his plate.

"Is this your first dig?" Jake asked her.

Elizabeth nodded. "I'm really looking forward to it."

"Yeah, me too," said Jake. "I want to specialize in this kind of work in a couple of years. Eastern Indian archaeology, I mean."

"Not me," said Milo. "You guys could dig all day and find nothing to work with. Now in forensic anthro we start out with a body, so there's no sense of futility."

Jake winked at Elizabeth. "Why do you hang out with this ghoul?"

Elizabeth smiled. "It's never dull. So you're interested in Eastern Indian cultures. Tell me, are you disappointed by the Cullowhee?"

Milo started to laugh, and Elizabeth expected to hear another tepee joke, but Jake answered, "I knew what to expect. I'm from western North Carolina, and the Cullowhees are pretty well known up here in the mountains because of the Moonshine Massacre."

"The *what?*"

"Shh! I think Dr. Lerche is ready to start. I'll tell you later."

Comfrey Stecoah, who had spent most of the meal conversing jovially with various cooks but eating little, was beginning the meeting. He rapped on the table for silence and waited until the assemblage had seated themselves in chairs or on the floor.

"Like to thank the reverend for the use of the church, even though he's not here to receive it." He glanced at the bewildered faces of the visitors and decided that further explanation was in order. "Preacher works in the towel factory and only comes back here on weekends. Now, most of you'uns know that these people are here to save our land from the strip miners." This exaggeration drew scattered applause and a startled look from Lerche. Ignoring this, Comfrey continued: "The professor here is going to talk about what he's doing, and I wanted you all to hear him out so that if any reporters or tourists was to ask you, you'd have your facts straight. So you mind what he says." He sat down, motioning for Lerche to come forward and leading a ripple of polite applause.

Alex Lerche blinked at the brown faces staring up at him from a rainbow of polyester. Knowing that he could not use technical jargon with this audience inhibited him. He gripped the wooden Bible stand, which had been set on a card table for an improvised lectern, straightened his tie, and said diffidently: "This is the last time you'll see me dressed up." The laughter the line always drew from college audiences was not forthcoming. With a slight cough, Lerche began again. "As you know, the purpose of this dig is to find out who you are, so to speak. Now as I told Mr.

Stecoah when he asked me to do this, I am not an expert on Eastern Indians. I did my early work with Plains Indians, but my specialty is forensic anthropology, so I do a lot of consulting work with law enforcement agencies."

Briefly he explained his work and how the technology used to identify murder victims could be applied to the identification of the bodies in the old cemetery. The blank faces of the audience made him wonder if they understood, or were even listening. As he talked, he studied their features: green eyes, brown eyes, dark hair of every variation, every shape of face. The Cullowhees couldn't have been as isolated as they seemed. From the look of them, they had originated the traveling-salesman jokes. Still, these people were not his concern; it was their ancestors he must identify, and if his theory was correct, they were very special people indeed. He found himself looking at Mary Clare's upturned face, and for a moment he forgot where he was. Perhaps they could go for a walk later. With an effort of will, he returned his attention to the lecture.

"Since I was asked to help the Cullowhees, I have been doing some studying of the archaeology of this region, and I have a theory about your origins. Mind you! It's just a theory at this stage." The excitement in his voice belied his warning. "Now, as some of you may know, the Cherokees were not the original inhabitants of the Southern mountains." From the startled faces of his listeners, Lerche could see that they had not known—but they wanted to hear more. "The Cherokees were a branch of the Iroquois tribe who invaded this area around four hundred years ago. There were other tribes here before them. The Algonkians and the Croatans were along the coastline, and a Siouan tribe occupied the Piedmont. We know something about these tribes from the writ-

61

ings of European settlers. But the people of the Southern highlands were never seen by the colonists. By the time Europeans got to this part of the country, these first people had vanished and this land was the Cherokee nation."

The room was unusually quiet. He had them now.

"Now, nobody knows anything about those first Indians. Not their name, their language—nothing. The only traces of them are some bits of pottery made of limestone and crushed quartz. Anthropologists have divided up the Southeast into different regions according to the tribes which occupied them. This area is Zone Six, and these people are known simply as the Zone Six people because nobody knows what else to call them. They are a complete mystery." He paused for effect. "I think you might be what's left of them."

Elizabeth thought that the cheering and applause might have gone on for half an hour, but for the quelling effect of a late arrival. Like the bad fairy at the christening, she later described it. She had been wondering how to waylay Comfrey Stecoah after the meeting to ask about Amelanchier, when the sudden silence brought her back to the present. All heads were turned to the doorway, where a wiry little man in gray work clothes stood scowling at them. Although he was not particularly large or powerful looking, the man's malevolence chilled the room.

"I reckon anybody can address this prayer meeting," he remarked to no one in particular. He looked around as if waiting for a challenge, but received none. "Don't nobody bother to give me the minutes of the meeting, because I know what's going on. The people of this valley stand to make good money by cooperating with the mining company—and there's going to be jobs, too! But prosperity wouldn't suit certain people." He looked meaningfully at Comfrey.

"Guess some people think poor folks is easier to boss around. And they're willing to do some mighty ugly things to get their way." He pointed at Lerche, who looked confused and embarrassed. "Now I don't know what kind of Indian curse will befall those who do not respect the graves of our ancestors, and I don't know what the penalty for grave robbing is in this state, but I aim to find out. And in the meantime, I advise you outlanders to remember the Moonshine Massacre. We don't take kindly to meddlers up here, no sir."

As he turned to leave, he walked past the table where the slide projector was set up for use later in the lecture. Before anyone could stop him, he had stumbled—or lunged—into the table, sending the machine crashing to the floor. With that he was gone.

Elizabeth saw that the stout woman who planted love vines was seated in the row behind her. "Shouldn't somebody call the sheriff?" Elizabeth whispered.

The woman shrugged. "He's in Laurel Cove. All we got up here is a deputy."

"Well, couldn't you call him?"

The woman permitted herself a grim smile. "Honey, you was just a-looking at him."

CHAPTER FIVE

Dear Bill,

They can't arrest archaeologists for graverobbing, can they? Could you check your law books and get back to me on this?

Ditchdigger's hands may be the least of my problems on this dig. Night before last some guy named Bevel Harkness crashed Dr. Lerche's lecture (and his slide projector) and threatened us for interfering in this land business. Mr. Stecoah told Dr. Lerche that this Harkness guy owns property next to the land the mining company wants, and he thinks he can sell out to them and make a fortune. You should see him. He'd make your skin crawl. To top it all off, he's the deputy sheriff for this part of the county! I thought the deputy would be Mr. Stecoah, if anybody; but it turns out that he's only been back from the service a couple of years (career Army), and Harkness' term doesn't run out for another year. They're in some sort of power struggle for tribal leadership, I guess. The Stecoahs are respected because of Amelanchier (I was right about Comfrey; he's her son!), and the Harknesses' claim to fame is the Moonshine Massacre. (I'm coming to that.)

We're settled into an old wooden church near the gravesite, and there are six of us staying here: me; Milo (who is so businesslike you wouldn't recognize him); Dr. Lerche and his other grad student, Mary Clare (there may be something between them; I'm not sure yet—I *know* it's none of my business; shut up); and two undergrads, Victor

Bassington and Jake Adair. Victor is a creep who does nothing but brag about how much money his family has, how important his father-the-diplomat is, and what an expert *he* is because he worked on a dig in England when his father was stationed there. He is *so* boring! We fight not to have to sit next to him at meals. Jake, the other guy, is all right. He's from Swain County, North Carolina, and he doesn't talk about himself, which is a welcome change from Victor, but he knows a lot about this area. Last night he told us some mountain ghost stories and about the Moonshine Massacre. (I've written that up separately so I can keep a copy in case I take another folklore course. It's enclosed.)

I haven't had time to see Amelanchier yet, but Mr. Stecoah said it would be all right to visit her after work sometime. Maybe I'll go this afternoon, since it isn't my turn to do supper today.

We haven't made any discoveries yet, unless you count the sore muscles we didn't know we had. The first few days of an excavation consist of shoveling off topsoil and sifting it through a screen to check for bones, arrowheads, etc. When we get to the graves, my job will be to measure the skulls. Dr. Lerche taught me how on a lab specimen he brought, but he says it's tricky and he'll double-check my work. I haven't seen much of him or Milo. They've hooked up a microcomputer in a motel room in Laurel Cove, and they've spent most of their days tinkering with it while I'm out in the hot graveyard listening to Victor pontificate and Mary Clare run on about how wonderful Dr. Lerche is. I'm looking forward to the skulls. At least they won't talk all the time.

Martyred in the Name of Science,
Elizabeth

THE MOONSHINE MASSACRE
(Collected from Jake Adair)

The Cullowhee Indians of Sarvice Valley had
never been a particularly law-abiding group,
and they were known for moonshining. Because
of the prejudice against Indians in those days,
the deputy sheriff in charge of Sarvice Valley
was never a Cullowhee, but always a local resi-
dent appointed by the county sheriff. This practice changed after the Moonshine Massacre of
1953.

The deputy sheriff at that time was a Korean
War veteran, just back from overseas. One afternoon he was driving down one of the dirt roads
in Sarvice Valley and he passed a weathered old
mountain graveyard. Two miles down the road,
the deputy realized why the image of that graveyard was still stuck in his mind: it hadn't been
there before he went off to war. When he went
back to investigate, he found that none of the
names on those old stones were familiar to him
either. Suddenly he noticed convection currents
coming from a fencepost beside the cemetery. A
few minutes' examination revealed the secret of
the old graveyard: it was an elaborate cover for
a moonshine operation. One enterprising Cullowhee had gone north with his truck (probably
on a moonshine run) and had seen an old cemetery being broken up for a building project. He'd
bought a truckload of old tombstones and set
them up on a hillside in Sarvice Valley on top of
an underground distillery. The vent pipe was
disguised as a fencepost. Unfortunately, the deputy did not live long enough to report his discov-

ery. The moonshiner saw him sneaking around the graveyard and shot him in the back.

When the deputy did not report back to the sheriff's department, searchers were sent out to look for him, and they didn't come back either. The moonshiner had decided that the best way to have a convincing cemetery was to provide a body for each tombstone. He buried the deputy under one of the headstones and was looking forward to furnishing the rest of the graves with likely passersby. This exercise in verisimilitude was finally halted by the Cullowhees themselves. The sheriff had called off the investigation due to lack of volunteers for further search parties, when a member of the Harkness family showed up in Laurel Cove and volunteered to bring the moonshiner to justice in exchange for the job of deputy. Harkness later claimed that his reason for doing so was the fact that the next grave to be filled was that of a small child, and he was afraid that the moonshiner might be a stickler for accuracy. Some of the Cullowhees claim that the Harkness' tendency to bully people was also a factor in their desire to become the law in Sarvice Valley.

After that the deputy job stayed in the Harkness family until 1972, when an obstinate sheriff insisted on appointing his nephew as the deputy of Sarvice Valley. Two weeks later the nephew disappeared and was never found. The Harkness family resumed the job and has kept it to the present day.

"Here's another skull for you, Elizabeth," said Jake, adding a carefully tagged specimen to the wooden crate in front of her. The rest of the remains were placed in separate cardboard boxes to be reburied later when the study had been completed.

67

The tag ensured that the skull would be reunited with the correct set of bones.

"I don't suppose it could be Victor's," grumbled Elizabeth, setting down the one she had been measuring.

Jake laughed. "What's he done now?"

"The usual. We were talking about folk medicine, and he said that his great-grandfather invented penicillin in the 1880s but never bothered to market it."

"Well ... it *could* be true."

"Oh, sure, it could. And Princess Diana might have babysat for his little brother; and he might have had a dream about a body walled up in a church tower and told the authorities about it, and they investigated and found one—"

"He said that?"

"He did. He says he has the pictures at home to prove it. They're in the same album with the snapshots of his white pony with the horn in its forehead."

"Old Victor has had an interesting life, hasn't he?" smiled Jake.

"Probably not. I expect he's had exactly the sort of life he looks like he's had. He's an overweight nerd with no particular talent who wants to be the center of attention, so he's trying to be as interesting as possible. Instead of getting mad at him, I should feel sorry for him. But he is so exasperating!"

"I know. You can't catch him in a lie. He once told me that Geronimo was Chief of the Seminoles, and I told him he was crazy. Finally I went to the library and photocopied the encyclopedia entry that said Geronimo was an Apache."

"How could he argue with that?"

"I made the mistake of letting him read the article. It said that after the U.S. Cavalry captured Geronimo, he was imprisoned in Florida. Victor swore that the Seminoles made him an honorary

68

chieftain then. He claimed to have a book that said so."

"At home, of course."

"Of course. Naturally, he couldn't come up with the title or author. I know what you mean about him. I wanted to strangle him that time. But you'll get used to him. Pretty soon you won't believe a word he says, and it won't bother you at all."

"Shh! Here he comes."

Victor Bassington, blissfully unaware that he had been the topic of discussion, waddled up to Jake and Elizabeth for no apparent reason other than the possibility of hijacking a conversation. His round face had the look of damp cheese, and his squinting in the sunlight made him look even more piggy than usual. "Jake, is it your turn to cook tonight? I wanted to remind you that I'm allergic to onions."

"I'm not likely to forget," sighed Jake.

"I may also be coming down with sun poisoning," Victor announced with mournful satisfaction. "Since Dr. Lerche has pitched a tent up here to store the finds in, and since he isn't around to use it himself, maybe he'd let me work in it."

"I wouldn't ask if I were you," Jake advised him. "Mary Clare's the site manager, and you know how she feels about delicate fieldworkers."

"She really is most unsympathetic. In England, when I worked with Heinrich Schliemann—"

"Ah-ha!" yelled Jake, pointing his finger disconcertingly close to Victor's nose. "Heinrich Schliemann died in 1890. I've got you!"

Victor blinked innocently at the finger. "Of course he did, Jake. I was going to say Heinrich Schliemann III, who is with the Royal Archaeological Society. Very nice fellow. But you may be right about Miss Gitlin. I suppose I'll have to brave it out until I drop." Mopping his forehead with a rumpled white handkerchief, he ambled off in the direction of the water jug.

Jake was grinding his teeth. "Now, I *know* there is no Heinrich Schliemann III in the Royal Archaeological Society, but in order to prove it, I'd have to find a *Dictionary of National Biography* or a membership list, and by the time I'm in a position to do that, I'll have forgotten the whole argument, or else he'll swear he didn't say it."

"I thought it didn't bother you any more," said Elizabeth in a carefully neutral tone.

"I was plainly mistaken," snapped Jake. "Someday, somehow, Victor Bassington is going to play Mr. Know-It-All to the wrong person, and he's going to get nailed to the wall with the facts. I just hope I'm there to lead the cheers."

"Good luck," smiled Elizabeth. "By the way, I may be late for supper tonight. I'm going to see Amelanchier after work. What are you cooking anyway?"

"I don't know, but there'll be onions in it; I promise you that." Jake picked up his trowel and headed back to the trenches.

Despite the painstaking precautions taken to filter the soil and check for unexpected finds, the work at the gravesite had gone unusually well. The four daytime volunteers were diligent workers who made up in enthusiasm what they lacked in experience. By the beginning of the third day, the site tent contained several boxes to be analyzed by Dr. Lerche, and Elizabeth had been able to practice her measuring techniques on eight new skulls. She was not convinced that her results were accurate, but her skill in using the instruments increased as she became accustomed to working with the grisly objects.

Elizabeth examined the latest acquisition—missing quite a few teeth for one as young as the cranial lines indicated—and decided that it was too late in the day to begin another measurement. This one could wait until morning. Perhaps by then Dr. Lerche would have finished his computer work and could double-check her original findings. If she hurried, she would have time to find Amelanchier and get acquainted before supper, leaving the rest of the evening free to spend with Milo.

Elizabeth stowed the crate in a corner of the site tent. "I just put my folks to bed," she told Mary Clare. "Do you need me for anything else?"

Mary Clare shook her head. "I'm about ready to pack it in myself. Maybe the guys will be back from town by now."

"Well, if they are, tell Milo I'll see him later. I'm going to find the Wise Woman of the Woods."

"More power to you," laughed Mary Clare. "I've got all the wise guys I can stand right here."

Although she had acquired a certain regional reputation, Amelanchier Stecoah was by no means easy to find. Outlanders seeking her advice had to park their cars at the church and follow a footpath through the woods, which, after a twenty-minute walk, mostly uphill, stopped in a clearing sheltered by a wooded ridge. At the end of the path, a crudely hand-lettered sign, the twin of the one on the highway, proclaimed: WISE WOMAN OF THE WOODS LIVES HERE. Smaller printing below advised: "If Door Locked, Ring Yard Bell or Rad a Note." A large brass bell was mounted on a post in front of an unpainted wooden shack. Elizabeth decided to try the porch door before ringing the bell.

"Hello?" she called out. "Anybody home?"

"Just got back!" answered a cheerful voice from within. "Come on in."

Elizabeth edged her way past an old wooden icebox and a cardboard box full of letters. The room was small and crowded, but the sprightly old lady in jeans and a denim workshirt was no martyr to poverty. Her eyes sparkled behind gold-rimmed glasses, and she jumped up to greet Elizabeth.

"And who might you be?" she asked in a tone suggesting that she'd be pleased to meet you whatever the answer.

Elizabeth introduced herself and explained that she was with the dig arranged by Amelanchier's son.

The old lady nodded at the mention of Comfrey's name. "He's the ambitious one of the bunch. Allus was."

"He said that it would be all right for me to visit with you. I'm very interested in herbs."

"I reckon you came to the right place then. Will you be wanting to go out gathering? I was just fixing to go get me some ginseng."

Elizabeth's eyes widened. Ginseng had been discussed in reverent tones in her folk medicine class. Hailed as a cure for everything from the common cold to cancer, it sold for $140 a pound for export from the Orient. "Do you think you'll find any?"

Amelanchier snorted at such a tomfool question. "We got a woods full of poplar trees. That's where it grows. 'Course we'll find some. Pick up that basket and follow along."

She led the way past a small shed beside her house, picking her way up the ridge through underbrush and around fallen logs. "Now you only want to pick the old plants," she told Elizabeth, lecturing as she walked. "Them young ones won't bring much nohow. Their roots are no bigger'n a peanut. And another thing: when you pick sang—ginseng, you folks call it—you always want to pick off that red berry that grows between the twigs, and you want to plant it. If you do that, why, there'll be a plant growing there the next time you go a-hunting it."

Elizabeth nodded, wishing she'd had the sense to bring a notepad with her. "How did you learn so much about wild plants?"

"Handed down in my family," said the old woman. She stooped to examine a small three-branched plant near the base of a tree. "My grandfather did the root medicine when I was a girl, and he taught me. Indians allus been close to the land. You know how there come to be healing plants in the first place?"

Elizabeth shook her head. She knelt beside Amelanchier and watched her uproot the small plant and carefully rebury the strawberrylike fruit.

"You want to watch how you kneel down out here in the woods," Amelanchier warned her. "Those copperheads blend right in with the underbrush. And you oughtn't to jump up quick like that, neither. Slow, steady movements is the best. Got to look out for snakes this time of year; bears mostly minds their own business. Animals aren't our friends, though, the way the plants are. That's how the healing plants come about. Back in olden times, when people could still talk to other living things and be talked back to, there was peace among us. But by and by, man began to get above hisself, wanting bearskins to keep him warm, and deer meat for supper, fish for fertilizer. Man became a danger to his fellow creatures. So all the animal folk of the world had a meeting and decided that something would have to be done about it."

"What did they do?"

Amelanchier dropped another root into the basket. "They brought disease into the world. The bear clan called down rheumatism on every hunter who killed without apologizing to the hunted one, and the deer people wished influenza and colds on those who were ungrateful for the animal hides that kept them warm. Pretty soon every beast and bird had come up with some ailment or another to wish on brother man, till it looked like there wouldn't be a soul to survive it."

"What did man do about it?"

"Wasn't nothing he could do. That would have been the end of us if it hadn't been for the fact that the plants were our friends. When they heard all these awful things being called up by the animal clans, they decided to help man out. So every tree, shrub,

73

grass, herb, moss—every growing thing decided that it would cure one of those evils. And they do, right down to this day. And when you learn which plant cures which evil—why, you're practicing medicine."

"So plants are our friends," mused Elizabeth, looking at the basket of roots.

"Yep. That's why I named every one of my young'uns after one. There's Laurel and Stargrass and Yarrow and Comfrey. He's my youngest, Comfrey is. Rest of 'em went off and got jobs in the big city. Reckon they'll be back when they get to be my age."

"Does Comfrey live with you?" asked Elizabeth, thinking of the tiny cabin.

Amelanchier smiled. "He couldn't hardly stand all the company I have. No, Comfrey's got him a little place down in the valley. He comes up to see me, though, 'bout ever' day or so. He sure is worried about this mining business the Harknesses are pushing for. He reckons it'll come to us losing the whole valley."

"We're not going to let that happen," Elizabeth assured her.

"Now how do you'uns aim to prove that we're entitled to the land? We don't have proof like the Cherokees got—stuff that looks good in a museum for the tourists. We come from the Unaka people, and them folks in Washington ought to take our word for it."

Elizabeth smiled at Amelanchier's idea of the workings of the federal government. She explained the basics of forensic anthropology, and the amazing process of determining age, sex, and race from the examination of a skull. In her enthusiasm, Elizabeth sounded much more expert than she actually was, but Amelanchier did not seem particularly impressed. She continued to scour the ground with a practiced eye, occasionally uprooting a small plant or picking a few leaves from a shrub.

"I'm doing the skull measurements myself!" said Elizabeth triumphantly.

"And you can tell all that?" murmured Amelanchier politely.

"Well, no," Elizabeth admitted. "Dr. Lerche can, of course. I just make measurements for him to check over later. So far he hasn't had time to look at them. He's setting up a computer in Laurel Cove."

Amelanchier straightened up and looked at the fading sky. "I reckon we ought to be starting back," she announced. "You come on back with me, and we'll talk some more about plants if you've a mind to. Is there anything in particular you'd like to know?" She eyed Elizabeth appraisingly. "I've got a sody cure that'll take weight off'n anybody."

Elizabeth blushed. "I'd like to hear it. I wish I could get another one of our diggers up here to see you. He's allergic to *everything*. Food, dust, bees, cats—everything! Do you have any medicine that would help that?"

"Why, ginseng ought to help some with it. I'll give you some of my powdered stock, and you take it back there to your camp and burn it, and make your friend inhale the smoke."

"Is it expensive?" asked Elizabeth doubtfully. She knew that ginseng brought fabulous prices, and that Victor was not worth a fraction of such an expenditure.

"Shoot far," scoffed Amelanchier. "I don't charge nothing. Plants just grow wild in the woods, don't they? They don't cost me nothing. Now, how would you like to stay for supper? I got a coon Comfrey shot laying up in my freezer, and we could have him with beans and cornbread."

Elizabeth hesitated. "It's very kind of you to ask me, but I've never ... I mean, what does raccoon taste like?"

"Just like bear!" was Amelanchier's instant reply.

CHAPTER SIX

THE MOONLIGHT did not illuminate the gravesite. From the granite ridge above, it looked like a large black square set down among the trees.

"I don't guess you can tell too much from here," said Mary Clare.

"I didn't come up here to look at it," Alex answered. "But I've inspected at closer range. You're doing a fine job as site manager."

"I enjoy it, Dr.—Alex."

He looked up at the night sky. "This whole experience of roughing it out here makes me feel young again. You know, when I was still a grad student, Tessa and I used to spend summers in the desert . . ." He stopped, realizing that Mary Clare had stiffened at the mention of his wife's name. "I guess those days are gone," he finished lamely.

Mary Clare touched his arm. "They don't have to be."

"It's not the same any more. When you're first starting out, you think you're going to be another Darwin. Revolutionize the field. But after a while, you're like those poor beasts in the La Brea Tar Pits: you're bogged down in mortgages and lectures and bridge games."

"I know, Alex, but it shouldn't be like that. What you need is someone who cares about your work instead of just your salary."

Lerche winced. He'd forgotten how melodramatic people could sound when they were courting. She's very young, he thought. But isn't that how I wanted to feel—young again? Suddenly—Alex wasn't quite sure how—he was holding her. An inborn urge to caution made him ask, "Won't the others be wondering about us?"

"They'll think we're working," whispered Mary Clare, without really considering it. "Shhh!"

"Hello!" said Elizabeth loudly to all the people she expected to find in the Sunday school room. A moment later, when she looked around, she saw that the only people present were Jake, reading a book, and Victor, who was working on a scale drawing of the site. "Where are Dr. Lerche and Mary Clare?"

"Out necking," said Jake, turning a page. "You want dinner?"

Elizabeth shook her head. "I had dinner with Amelanchier. Where's Milo?"

"He came back to eat and waited around for you, but when Dr. Lerche went off with Mary Clare, he said he was going back to work on the computer, and he stomped out."

Elizabeth sat down at the table beside Jake. "Milo's been awfully edgy lately," she mused.

"Like a bear," nodded Victor without looking up. "Too much caffeine, I expect."

"No, I think it's something—emotional," said Elizabeth, groping for the word. "He seems upset about something."

Jake eyed her warily. "This is an interesting book I'm reading," he remarked. "It's about the Cherokees."

"If you're interested in Indian lore, you ought to go up and talk to Amelanchier. I went out gathering with her this afternoon, and she told me all sorts of wonderful stories. Oh, and, Victor, she sent you an allergy cure."

Victor looked up suspiciously from his map. "She what?"

"I told her that you were allergic to the immediate

77

world, and she said that if you will inhale the smoke of this ginseng—what are you laughing at?"

Victor favored her with a condescending smile. "My parents have spent thousands of dollars taking me to the best allergy specialists in Washington. I don't need the service of the local witch doctor, thank you."

"You never know, Victor," grinned Jake. "After all, penicillin started out as bread mold. Maybe she has an old Indian miracle drug."

"You don't have to tell *me* about Indians, Jake. My great-grandmother was a Cherokee princess." With a self-righteous nod, Victor returned to his drawing.

Jake sighed. "I've been waiting for that one," he whispered to Elizabeth.

Elizabeth braced herself for another shouting match, and she was surprised when none was forthcoming. Jake turned again to his book, apparently unaffected by Victor's latest claim. She walked to the window, looking for the shine of headlights that would signal Milo's return, but the road was dark. Since she wasn't hungry and didn't owe anyone a letter, she began to wander about the room, peering over Victor's shoulder at his drawing and studying the plaques and pictures on the wall. A sepia photograph of some bygone Sunday school class attracted her attention.

"That's funny!" she said aloud.

"What?" asked Jake, turning a page.

"This picture must be fifty years old judging from the outfits they're wearing, but the people look just the same."

"Mountain witch woman discovers elixir to keep people from aging," Jake intoned without looking up.

"Idiot! That's not what I meant. Of course they're different people, but they're just as much of a hodge-podge as the ones today. Blonds, people with dark straight hair, people with dark kinky hair, light ones, dark ones. I thought that the farther back you went, the more pure Indian they'd look."

"Not the Cullowhees," Jake told her cheerfully. "They've always been like that."

Elizabeth considered this. "What do you think of them?" she asked. "Are they the Zone Six people?"

Jake shook his head. "I'm no expert, but for what it's worth, I think Lerche's wrong about the Cherokees being recent invaders. I think they've been in these mountains all along."

"That's not what Amelanchier told me. She—"

"Where's Alex?"

They turned to see Milo standing in the doorway, pale and breathless. Jake and Elizabeth glanced at each other, and silently agreed to an edited version of the truth.

"He's out walking," Elizabeth answered lightly. "He should be back soon. Come in and let me tell you about—"

"Not now, Elizabeth!" snapped Milo, slamming the door behind him.

Victor looked up, disturbed by the noise. "What was that all about?"

"Trouble, I expect," Jake answered.

"If there isn't, there's going to be," said Elizabeth grimly.

Milo ran along the dark path to the gravesite. He knew the way well enough to dodge tombstones and tree branches with only the moon to light the way. He was too worried to consider the etiquette involved in interrupting a love tryst or to let his fancy make ghosts of the graveyard's shadows. Milo had enough to worry about already.

He stopped just short of the excavation trench and looked around. There was no one in sight, and the tent was dark, as he expected. Everything seemed to be in order, though. He decided to let them find him.

"Alex!" he shouted, cupping his hands to his mouth. "Where are you? It's Milo!"

Having made that announcement, Milo sat down on a rock to wait. Maybe he shouldn't have been so short with Elizabeth, but a crisis is no time for remembering one's manners. He would explain it to her later, and he hoped that she wouldn't make a big deal out of it. He sighed. One romance gumming up the works was enough for any dig. After a few silent minutes, he thought he heard footsteps running through the trees in the direction of the church. A moment later, Alex appeared in the clearing.

"Milo? What on earth's the matter?"

"Somebody trashed the computer," said Milo grimly.

"Trashed—when?"

"Earlier tonight. I drove back to town after supper to add some more data to the program, and when I got to the motel room, I found the disks had been ripped apart and the computer screen was smashed."

"Damn!" Alex motioned him down the path toward the church. "We'll have to report this, of course."

"I already did. The guy on duty at the sheriff's office took down the information, but he didn't seem too upset. I take it the Cullowhees aren't too popular around here."

"I'll go and see them in the morning. Then I guess we'd better see about replacing the equipment. Damn!"

Milo nodded. "How many days is this going to cost us?"

"I don't know. A couple. I have duplicate disks back at the university, thank God! And we ought to be able to borrow another computer from the department for the time being."

"Okay. Do you want me to drive back to campus tomorrow and pick up the replacements?"

"No, I'll go. Do you have any idea who did this, Milo? Did it look like a burglary? Kids, maybe?"

"I'd say whoever did this knew something about computers. Enough to go after the disks, anyway."

Alex grunted. "From now on, one of us stays at the motel room on guard. This isn't going to happen again."

Alex sat on the top step of the church, watching the sky grow light. It was too early to go to the sheriff's office, even too early to start breakfast; but he hadn't been able to sleep. The smashing of the computer was probably a senseless act of violence, but he couldn't escape the feeling that it was an omen. He was taking it personally. He watched the trees become distinct shapes in the graying light. The cold light of day, he thought, smiling to himself. It seemed silly to think such things in daylight. Obviously, someone didn't want the Cullowhee study to continue, but that wasn't what troubled him. That was a minor annoyance. He kept feeling that there was some other message in the incident. A twinge in his lower back made him wince. He missed his bed at home and the luxury of long hot showers, which would loosen his muscles. Apparently the rigors of excavation work taxed muscles that racquetball left untoned. He wasn't as young as he used to be; there was no getting away from that. Still, it was strange that, after last night, he should be up at dawn thinking of Tessa.

Why had he volunteered to go back to campus for the disks? If he went home, there might be a renewal of the cold war that existed between himself and Tessa. Surely he wanted to stay with Mary Clare—especially after last night. He shrugged. There was no point in worrying about that now. He would go back to campus for the disks, and sort out his feelings later.

Elizabeth appeared at the opening of the tent holding a cardboard box. "Excuse me," she said with frosty politeness. "I wonder if you would have time to look at these now? I have done twenty already and no one has checked my work."

Milo looked up from his column of figures. Alex had taken the van to go to the sheriff's office in town, and then he was going to drive back to the university. Milo, in charge until Alex's return, was feeling particularly harassed after listening to a recital of imagined illnesses by Victor, a request for more help in the third trench from Jake, and a cross-examination by Mary Clare on "what Alex said about his plans before he left." Elizabeth's chilling courtesy made it plain that there was trouble in that quarter as well.

Milo decided that he had better make time for this interview. "Look, Elizabeth, I know I've been cross lately, but—"

"Don't bother to explain," said Elizabeth coldly. "It spoils your image. Why don't you just go and eat a village?"

Milo sighed. "I'm sorry." He took the cardboard box from her with as much enthusiasm as he could muster. "Let's see what you've found."

Elizabeth brightened a little. "Okay. First I cleaned them off very carefully before taking any measurements."

"That's good. Those teeth are easy to lose."

"Excuse me, Milo!" Mary Clare was peering into the tent with a worried frown. "Can you come out here?"

"Uh . . . is it important?"

"Yes! Somebody from the sheriff's department is here about the computer. He wants to talk to the person in charge. I think it had better be you."

With a sigh of resignation, Milo set down the box

of skulls. "If it isn't one thing, it's another. We'll have to do this later, Elizabeth."

She managed a weak smile. "Sure, Milo."

Near the first trench, a short, thin man in a khaki uniform was bent over the transit instrument, fiddling with the alignment.

Milo hurried toward him, intending to distract the man from the delicate instrument as politely as possible. "Hello there! May I help you? I'm Milo Gordon, the person in charge here."

"Naw, you ain't," leered the man, turning as he spoke. "I'm in charge in these parts."

Milo recognized him as the disrupter of Dr. Lerche's slide presentation. "You wanted to see me?" asked Milo in tones of careful politeness and understated dislike.

"Depends." The man shrugged. "I'm Deputy Sheriff Bevel Harkness, here on police business. Where's your boss, boy?"

Milo's mouth twitched with annoyance. "Dr. Lerche is gone for the day. I'm in charge now."

"Okay. I hear you'uns got a crime to report. Would that be other than this one?" He nodded toward the excavation with a taunting smile.

Milo could see no point in embarking on a shouting match with the deputy. The chances of getting a competent investigation of the vandalism depended upon maintaining good relations with the investigators. He said: "Last night before eight o'clock, someone broke into the motel room we rented in Laurel Cove, and they damaged our computer and destroyed the disks."

"Don't that beat all?" Harkness remarked. "How do you reckon they got in?"

"Those doors didn't look any too sturdy to me," said Milo. "I expect a credit card would have jimmied the lock. Don't you think you ought to investigate the scene instead of asking me?"

Harkness took the criticism calmly. "They sent me

out to talk to you, being that you're in Sarvice Valley, which is my section. Reckon the other stuff will get done as well. I got a form here." He produced a notebook and pencil and proceeded to read off questions, most of which seemed to concern the complainant's age, occupation, and permanent address. Milo answered them in tones of decreasing civility. "That ought to about do it," Harkness said at last. "Will y'all be closing this thing down now?"

Milo grinned. "Oh, no, Mr. Harkness. We'll be back in business by tomorrow."

"Now, what do you want to go and do that for?" asked Harkness in a pained voice. "All those people want is to get themselves declared an Indian tribe so they can sit back and collect government benefits like a bunch of pet squirrels. And you folks are helping them get a free ride. It's going to cost the taxpayers a bundle."

"I thought you were a Cullowhee yourself."

"Reckon so," Harkness allowed. "But that don't mean I want to get by without working. I don't need no handouts."

"The only thing these people seem concerned with is saving this valley from strip mining, Mr. Harkness."

"Well, I can't stand around here all day," said Harkness, pocketing his notepad. "Y'all just watch out for that old Indian curse when you go disturbing the dead."

"We will certainly watch out," said Milo carefully.

Elizabeth spent most of the morning in the shade of an oak tree, rechecking measurements and recording her findings legibly in a spiral notebook. By now the skulls had become so familiar that they had lost their grotesqueness, and with it their ability to distract her. They had ceased to be "real" to her in the same way the money she once handled as a cashier had become green pieces of paper after a few days of familiarity. The money had no value because it was not hers to spend; likewise, the skulls had no power over her emotions because she had come to know them as objects and she had never known them as people. She was, therefore, just as surprised as Mary Clare when the latest addition to the collection reduced her to tears.

"Good Lord!" said Mary Clare, setting it carefully in the box. "What's one more in this bunch? Why wouldn't you pick it up?"

"It's so small," said Elizabeth faintly.

"Oh, that."

"All the others had been just...specimens, I guess. And, look, they're missing teeth, and they have hardly any suture closures, which means they were pretty old. But this one is a child."

"Well...a hundred years ago."

"I know. But there's still something sad about a life that never had a chance to happen. Was it a boy or a girl?" Elizabeth looked closely at the tiny skull, trying to imagine a face for it.

"No one could tell you," said Mary Clare softly. "I don't know much about this myself, but I do remember Alex saying that if a child is younger than twelve, you can't tell sex differences from skeletal remains. Basically there *aren't* any differences at that age."

"I wonder how it died."

"Fever, most likely. Typhoid from bad water, or influenza. Cholera, maybe. Even an infected finger. It was easy to die back then."

Elizabeth shuddered.

Mary Clare looked at her closely. She didn't hold with catering to delicate people on a dig, but Elizabeth had been working hard. She wondered if this touch of nerves had been brought on by the skulls or by the situation with Milo.

"Look, Elizabeth, why don't you take a break? In

fact, I could use one myself—in case you'd like to talk."

Elizabeth sighed. She wouldn't have minded talking about Milo, but she didn't think it would be appropriate to do so with one of his colleagues. "I'll be all right, thanks," she said, forcing a smile.

"Oh, sure you will," said Mary Clare. "Milo's all right. He just needs to get used to dealing with live people, that's all. Just like you need to get used to dead ones." She pointed to the box of skulls. "How are you liking your work?"

"Fine. It's interesting and . . . you get used to it. I'm just not sure I'm doing it right. Milo doesn't seem to have time to check my calculations. I don't suppose you—"

"Nope! Don't know a tibia from a soupbone. My specialty is excavation, soil layers, stuff like that. I know how you feel about waiting around, but that computer business has thrown us for a loop. Anyhow, Alex should be back tomorrow. I'll make sure he checks your work first thing." She sighed. "I sure do miss him."

Before Elizabeth could think of a suitable reply, they were distracted by the sound of someone approaching from the woods. After a few moments, a middle-aged woman wearing a blue print dress and boy's high-topped sneakers appeared in the clearing. Elizabeth recognized her as the woman they had talked to at the church social.

"Hello!" Mary Clare called out. "You're our first tourist! Want a look around?"

The woman looked embarrassed. She glance at the box beside them and looked away. "I didn't rightly come to do that," she said. "Reckon I might be kin to some o' them people you're a-digging up."

"We're very careful with them," said Elizabeth earnestly. "And they'll be put right back as soon as the study is over."

"I know. Comfrey Stecoah explained the rights of

it to us 'fore he asked you'uns to come. I ain't put out about it; I just don't 'specially want to watch you a-doing it. I brought you some tomatoes from my garden, though. Figured you might like to have some for lunch." She held out a paper bag to Elizabeth.

Elizabeth was touched at such a gesture of friendliness from a stranger. "Thank you very much," she said. "Would you like to stay and join us?"

The woman shook her head. "Thank you all the same. I just figured I'd bring these things to you gals. Least I could do." She hesitated. "You 'member them love vines I planted for you'uns?"

They nodded.

"Well, I reckon the sun musta got too hot fer 'em, poor old Alexander and Robert. They shriveled up and died, the both of 'em."

CHAPTER SEVEN

ALEX TAPPED his fingers against the steering wheel and stared up at the church. It looked cool and peaceful in the late-afternoon sunlight. Strange that he should be so reluctant to go in. It was six o'clock; they would all be in the Sunday school room having dinner—a flavorless concoction prepared on a hot plate. Alex wondered at his own distaste for the project. For the first time in his career, he resented having to leave his comfortable home, well-cooked meals, and especially his Posture-Perfect mattress. Roughing it had lost some of its glamour, perhaps in proportion to his own loss of youth. Or perhaps the real reason for his reluctance lay in the fact that he would have to face Mary Clare. He was going to feel like a fool, and he dreaded it. Even that stupid act of vandalism bothered him, although he didn't know why it should. If the Neanderthals had still been around, mightn't they have risen up in the caves of Lascaux and said, "Leave our dead alone!" If the protest over his work always existed in theory, why should he mind the expression of it?

The side door to the church opened, and he saw a figure in jeans standing on the porch. By the time he noticed the blond hair, which identified the person as Mary Clare, she had seen the van and was running toward it. Alex, who had planned to rehearse everything in his mind, had no idea what he was going to say.

Mary Clare rested her elbows on the van's open window and peered in happily at Alex. "I'm real glad you're back," she beamed. "I've been looking out for you since five or so. How was your trip?"

"Fine. Is everything all right here?"

"Yep. Milo spent most of yesterday and today either at the sheriff's office or guarding that motel room with Comfrey Stecoah, though what they meant to accomplish by that, I'm sure I don't know."

"Probably a symbolic gesture," said Alex.

"Well, the work is coming along fine. Do you want to go up to the site and take a look?"

He nodded. "After supper." He wasn't hungry, but eating the tasteless food in the common room would postpone his having to be alone with Mary Clare. He followed her up the hill to the church, still wondering what to say.

Inside the Sunday school room, Victor Bassington was holding forth to a captive audience of diggers, who were bolting their food as quickly as possible in order to escape.

"Archaeology! The mysteries of the ages! That's why I'm studying it. Why was Machu Picchu abandoned? Why did the Neanderthals die out?"

"You'll never know," muttered Jake between mouthfuls of bread.

"Ah! Can we be sure? Science opens new doors every day. Take this Cullowhee mystery. Who are they? I think they came from the Orient—"

"I thought *all* Indians originally came from the Orient," Elizabeth put in.

"Ah, but *these* Indians seem more Oriental than most," said Victor without missing a beat. "Those skulls you're working with remind me very much of the skull of the Peking man I saw in England. Something about the shape—"

"That's very interesting," said Elizabeth politely. She hoped that her comment had distracted Victor from the sound of Jake's snickering.

"Yes, very interesting indeed," said Alex, who had

been standing in the doorway listening. "I should like to hear more."

Victor turned slowly, a blush creeping upward toward his ears. "Why, welcome back, Dr. Lerche. I was just talking about how interesting all this is."

"Yes, I heard you," said Alex evenly. "You mentioned seeing the skull of the Peking man. That must have been quite an experience for you. When was this?"

"While I was in England," Victor said in a much more subdued voice. "Two or three years ago."

"I see," said Lerche. "Was this in a museum, perhaps?"

Victor hesitated. "The ... ah ... British Museum. But I don't think they're there all the time. I believe it was a traveling exhibit. I guess I was just lucky to be visiting at the right time."

"Lucky," Lerche repeated sarcastically. "Oh, you were phenomenally lucky, Mr. Bassington. You saw the actual bones, not a plaster copy?"

"The actual bones," Victor agreed cautiously. "In a glass case, of course."

"Here it comes," whispered Jake to Elizabeth.

"I find it very interesting that you saw the skull fragments of *Sinanthropus pekinensis* two or three years ago in the British Museum. Do you know why I find that so interesting, Mr. Bassington?"

"Uh ... did you see them then too?" asked Victor hopefully.

"No—and neither did you. The remains of Peking man were found in China in 1929 and *they disappeared in China in 1939!* When the Japanese invaded Manchuria, the museum people entrusted them to soldiers who were supposed to get them to a safe place. The soldiers were captured and the bones were never found."

"Oh," said Victor in a small voice.

"I don't know why you have a compulsion to be an expert on things you know nothing about, but you're wasting your time, because no one will ever believe a word you say." He turned to the rest of the group. "All of you could stand to do a lot more studying and a lot less posturing. You're not scientists yet!" He left the Sunday school room, slamming the door behind him.

Mary Clare hurried to keep up with him. "He's had that coming," she said softly. "But it's not like you to do it in public thataway."

Alex grunted. "Where's Milo?"

"Well, he figured you'd be sending the new monitor up by bus, so he found out when the bus gets in and went down to wait for it. He'll be back soon. Are you going to the site? Because if you are, Elizabeth Mac-Pherson has a whole boxful of skulls already measured. She'd like you to check her work."

"All right."

Mary Clare hoped that if she could get Alex to talk, he would slow down and stop crashing through the woods like a wounded razorback. "Did you get the disks?" she called.

Alex turned to look at her. "My wife is bringing them," he said.

She looked at him saucer-eyed, then began to smile. "I guess you haven't told her yet, have you? But I don't think there'll be any problem if you just tell her what you're planning to do from now on."

"And what is that?" asked Alex quietly.

Mary Clare blushed. "Oh, I didn't mean about us. Though I reckon it might be kinder to tell her straight out. I meant what you were talking about the other night: about quitting the university and going off to be an independent archaeologist. Living in camps under the stars, doing whatever job takes your fancy . . ." She smiled, thinking how wonderful it was going to be.

"You want me to be a shovel bum?" Alex demanded. He sat down on a fallen log and began to laugh.

Mary Clare, who wasn't sure what the joke was—
or on whom—watched him nervously.

"I can't believe it. *A shovel bum.*"

"What's that, Alex?" she asked timidly.

"That, my dear, is a contract archaeologist who
digs up any site for a price. Antiquities bounty
hunters. Most of them lack advanced degrees, and
they aren't backed by those universities you scorn so
much. Who do you think pays for projects? Universities, that's who! And without their backing, you have
no professional standing in the field, and no one will
pay very much attention to your findings."

"But ... Schliemann found Troy on his own."

"We're not talking about a hundred years ago,
Mary Clare. I'm telling you that *today* the shovel
bums dig up a site with no research concept and
probably destroy evidence that a real scholar could
use. They simply take the money and run to the next
job. University backing is the only symbol of integ-
rity we've got. And you want me to throw it away!"
He shook his head. "You are just as bad as Victor.
You make childish plans based on something you
know nothing about."

"I'm sorry," she whispered.

Alex sighed. "I'm sorry, too. I'm afraid I haven't
been very realistic these past few weeks either, and
you misunderstood me. I didn't want to be a shovel
bum, Mary Clare. I wanted to be twenty-three
again." He tried not to look at her. "Do you understand?" he asked gently.

She nodded. "I guess so."

"Well, I have an interesting assignment for you. It
has to do with this project, and I think it would be
best for all of us if you took it."

"What is it?"

"You remember that research check I put in at the
library before we left? They've come up with something. It seems that MacDowell College has a diary
and some letters written by a woman from this area.

There may be something on the Cullowhees in her writings. It dates back a hundred years or so."

"And you want me to read through it? When will it get here?"

"It won't. It's in MacDowell's rare-manuscript collection, and they won't lend it out. You'll have to go to their library to examine the documents."

"You mean I have to leave?" wailed Mary Clare.

"It could be very important to the project," said Alex gently. "And I think it might be the best thing for all of us."

Mary Clare glared at him through tears. "I wish you were dead!" she screamed.

"Where is Milo?" muttered Elizabeth for the third time in as many minutes.

Jake sighed. "Do you think it would help any if he were here?"

"I feel as if I've wandered onto the set of a soap opera," she grumbled. "Victor just sits there glowering, and God knows what's wrong with Mary Clare. She keeps slamming things into a suitcase, and she's trying to pretend she's not crying."

"And we're trying to pretend we don't notice," Jake agreed.

"I wonder if she'd think I was being nosy if I went over there?" Elizabeth wondered.

"I think we ought to leave her alone," Jake replied. "We don't know her very well."

Victor glared at them from his worktable. "Will you two stop whispering? It is very distracting—and ill-mannered as well."

"We weren't talking about you, Victor," said Jake wearily.

"I didn't say you were, but I *am* trying to work. It's hard enough as it is, without your twittering in the background. That ugly scene tonight has given me a paralyzing migraine."

"It wasn't an ugly scene. Lerche caught you out,

that's all. Just admit you had it coming and forget about it."

"It was quite juvenile of him to pounce on me like that!" Victor insisted. "Cruel, in fact. It should have been obvious to him that I had made a slip of the tongue. Of course what I saw on exhibit was *Homo habilis*. That is what I *thought* I had said until he made such a scene about it."

"I expect he was upset over something else," said Elizabeth soothingly.

"No doubt. But he had no right to speak to me like that. None!" He stood up and shook his fist at a blank wall. "I think I shall go out for a while. Perhaps the fresh air will ease the pain in my head. Or perhaps I shall be bitten by a rattlesnake!"

"Have fun, Victor!" said Jake, stifling a grin.

Elizabeth watched him march to the door. "This dig is more of an adventure than I bargained for," she remarked. "Computer pirates, lovers' quarrels, violent arguments. Exhuming bodies is getting to be the dullest part of the project."

"I hope that changes," said Jake gloomily. "I'm a peace-loving man, myself."

"At least you're behaving normally, Jake. Milo is really edgy." Elizabeth saw the door open. "Shhh! I think he's coming in now."

A moment later she saw that it was not Milo, but Dr. Lerche who had come in. He stood at the door looking uncomfortable for a few moments. Mary Clare looked up from her packing, saw him, and walked out, nose in the air. He moved away from the door to let her pass, and walked over to Jake and Elizabeth.

"Where is Milo?"

"At the bus station. He said he'd be back at eight," Elizabeth offered.

Alex consulted his watch. "It's five after," he announced.

"Well, he isn't here," said Elizabeth. "Shall I send him up to the site when he arrives?"

"Yes, please do." Lerche seemed to be thinking of something else. He was looking at the old photographs on the walls. "I examined those skulls you did. I'm going back to the site. Send Milo as soon as he comes."

Before Elizabeth could ask him anything else about her work, he had hurried out again. "I wonder what that was about," she remarked.

"There's no telling," answered Jake. "It could be anything from untagged soil layers to a misplaced trowel. Don't worry. If you had done anything wrong, he would have told you."

"I guess so," said Elizabeth doubtfully. She thought it much more likely that Lerche would delegate problems of that sort to Milo, since she was his protégée on the dig. There seemed to be no point in worrying, though. She was a beginner, and she had done her best.

Since there seemed to be a lull in the theatrics of the Sunday school room, Jake returned to his book on Cherokee archaeology, and Elizabeth wrote up an account of her meeting with Amelanchier so that she would not forget what she had been told.

It was nearly nine o'clock when Mary Clare eased open the door to the Sunday school room. Her face was flushed and her hair disheveled, but she was no longer crying.

"I saw headlights on the road," she told Elizabeth. "I reckon that'll be Milo headed back."

"Oh, good!" cried Elizabeth, hurrying to the window.

"I'm glad you think so," snorted Mary Clare. "But you'd better watch out for those anthropologists. All they know how to work with is dead people, and dead people don't have feelings." She lifted her chin as if to prepare herself for cries of protest, but none were forthcoming. Jake had retreated into his book, and

Elizabeth, still peering out the window, wasn't listening.

In a calmer voice, Mary Clare said, "Y'all may as well know I'm leaving to do some literary research on this project. I guess Alex will site-manage himself."

"Here's the car!" cried Elizabeth.

"You didn't see Victor outside, did you?" Jake asked. "He went off a while ago announcing his intention of getting snakebit."

Mary Clare was relieved that they had not questioned her about her sudden plans for departure. She managed a grim smile. "No. I was out walking around. Victor can't have gone as far as I did; that would be *exercise.*"

"Excuse me. I'm looking for my husband."

Tessa Lerche stood in the doorway smiling politely. She wore beige canvas pants, an open-throated khaki shirt, and a red silk neckerchief—her concept of expedition chic. Her newly shingled hair would be easy to care for without the aid of the beauty parlor.

Mary Clare, who was wearing faded jeans and a blue T-shirt, looked appraisingly at Tessa and remarked, "You forgot your pith helmet."

"Dr. Lerche is up at the site," Jake put in quickly. "Would you like me to take you there? It isn't far."

"Sorry we can't call you a cab." Mary Clare smirked.

How very un-Southern! Elizabeth thought wildly. We're usually more polite to our enemies than we are to our friends.

Tessa, too, seemed taken aback by Mary Clare's hostile remarks. She eyed her carefully, as if waiting for an indication that this was all in fun. The other two occupants of the room, obviously students, looked embarrassed, she noted with satisfaction, but Mary Clare continued to stare. Tessa smiled, as winners can afford to, and said gently, "I understand you are leaving us, Mary Clare."

"I figured you put him up to it."

Tessa's smile faded. "No, dear, *you* did. You pushed." Dismissing the matter, she turned to Jake, as if being the only male present made him the person in charge. She fished the computer disks out of her canvas purse and held them up. "I have brought these for the computer," she announced brightly, in tones suggesting that the previous conversation with Mary Clare had not taken place. "My poor husband drove all the way back to campus to get them, and then he got so caught up with his mail and his laundry and whatnot, that he drove off without them." She laughed fondly, inviting them all to share her amusement in her absentminded professor. She neglected to mention that she had unobtrusively moved the disks out of sight and had not reminded him to take them. "So he called me from a gas station somewhere and asked me to bring them up here. So here I am!"

"Yes, ma'am," answered Jake warily. "Milo will be real glad to get them. Will you be staying the night? I mean, I'd be glad to bring your things up from the car."

Tessa's answer was addressed to Jake, but it was meant for Mary Clare. "Thank you, but that won't be necessary. Alex and I will be staying at a motel room in Laurel Cove. We feel it will be safer that way."

Nice double entendre, thought Elizabeth.

Jake shifted uncomfortably, sensing another outbreak of bickering. "Would you like me to take you up to the site? It's past dark, so Dr. Lerche should be quitting pretty soon. He doesn't like to work much by lantern light."

"I'm quite aware of that," said Tessa, courteously reinforcing her status as incumbent. "Yes, let's go and see him."

Outside a car horn honked.

Jake jumped up as if he had heard the bugle of the Seventh Cavalry. "That's Milo! He'll be happy to take

97

you up to the site. Dr. Lerche has been wanting to see him anyway."

"Who hasn't?" muttered Elizabeth.

Milo was careful to shine the flashlight on the path in front of Tessa. She had asked nervously about snakes when they started out, and even though he assured her that they had not seen any, she still walked with the tentative steps of one who is expecting to be ambushed. She had not spoken, except to make a few polite inquiries about the project, which Milo had answered in monosyllables. He was glad of the silence, much preferring the crickets' mindless chirp to Tessa's. The tedium of a day with the bureaucracy and the wait at the bus station-general store had exhausted him more than digging trenches ever did. He had taken the monitor back to the motel room and made sure it was working before hurrying back to the church to spend the evening with Elizabeth. He had not anticipated the melodrama that awaited him: his boss's wife and mistress staring each other down like angry cats.

Milo wondered what had transpired while he had been in Laurel Cove. It was embarrassing to see Alex entangled in such a situation. Detached and unemotional Alex! He wished he hadn't brought Elizabeth along on this dig. It could not have given her a very good impression of anthropologists. The thought that he had not been Prince Charming, either, flickered through his mind, but was dismissed in a flood of justification.

"Are we almost there?" asked Tessa.

"Almost."

"I don't want to fall into an open grave." She shuddered.

"There, see the light in the clearing? That's the lantern in the tent." Rather awkwardly, he took her wrist. "I'll show you how to get there, so you won't fall."

Tessa hung back. "Milo, I know this is silly ..."

The entire day had been a farce, Milo thought bitterly, but he waited for her to continue.

"Could you just ask Alex to put the skulls away before I go in? I know I sound terribly squeamish for an anthropologist's wife, but it's so dark and quiet out here." Her voice shook. "I don't think I could take much more."

"Sure," said Milo, relieved at being asked to do something that was merely stupid instead of embarrassing. "You wait here. I'll come back for you."

He walked the last fifteen feet across the cemetery to the tent. Whatever Alex had wanted to see him about would have to be postponed, he supposed. He wondered what it was, tempted to ask before he announced Tessa's presence to her husband. Milo pulled back the tent flap. "Hey, Alex ..."

Milo's years of studying forensic anthropology compared to this as a grainy out-of-date war movie might resemble actual combat. The outlines were similar, but the emotions were so lacking as to render the actual event unrecognizable. Part of Milo's mind noted the curious difference between the clinical reality of a deceased stranger on a stainless-steel table, and the newly murdered body of one's friend and colleague.

Alex Lerche lay slumped over his worktable with outstretched arms. Milo looked at the back of his head, and thought, "A broken bowl of Jell-O," wondering if the image made him less likely to throw up or more so. Beside Alex on the table lay a bloody stone tomahawk, the souvenir kind sold in Cherokee and made in Taiwan. It consisted of a real stone tied to a pine stick with red plastic threads, adorned with chicken feathers dyed lime green and orange. The sight would have been ridiculous but for the blood on the tomahawk and the line of Indian skulls jeering in the lantern light.

CHAPTER EIGHT

DANIEL HUNTER COLTSFOOT studied the wanted posters on the sheriff's bulletin board, trying to decide which of them to cover up with his craft fair announcement. Surely some victimless, drug-related offense could be obscured for a few days for such a worthy notice as the Nunwati Nature-Friends Herb and Craft Day. Daniel enjoyed telling people that Nunwati was the Cherokee word for medicine, and that even though none of their members was actually a Native American, they liked to think that they were Indian in spirit, keeping the old traditions alive with pottery works and leathercraft shops.

Coltsfoot and his girlfriend, Patricia Elf, ran a health food store in Laurel Cove, doing a thriving business among tourists who mistook them for Indians, an error which they did not discourage. Actually, Coltsfoot and Patricia were not even picturesque locals: he was from Baltimore, and she was a New Yorker, but they managed to obscure this with homespun outfits and colonial hairstyles. Daniel had even added Coltsfoot to the end of his name in an effort to sound more "ethno-regional," happily unaware that the coltsfoot plant went by another name in the eastern Appalachians. Behind his back the bemused locals referred to the plant and to Daniel himself as "Dummyweed." In their health food store they spoke reverently of Amelanchier Stecoah, and they liked to be thought colleagues of hers, but in fact she had taken no notice of them. Once Daniel had gone to see her about purchasing some ginseng, but she had declined to do business with them. That had been two years ago, when the Nunwati Nature-Friends were new to the area. Daniel thought that he might try again sometime, now that the group was more widely known. Their *Nunwati Newsletter* was selling well at the commercial campgrounds and from the lobby of the Cherokee Wigwam Motel. Futhermore, Daniel had attained a certain measure of respectability by becoming a deputy sheriff. He had not intended to join forces with the county law enforcement officials, but he was rather pleased at having had the honor thrust upon him. It had happened the previous fall when seven maximum-security prisoners overpowered a guard and escaped from a work detail across the mountains in East Tennessee. News of cars stolen and hostages taken had filled even the pages of the biweekly county newspaper, and the local radio station urged its listeners to take care, predicting that the convicts would soon be at their very doors.

Patricia Elf became so frightened at the thought of these marauders at large that she refused to work in the health food shop alone. After several days of confinement in the shop, Daniel decided that there must be a better way to pacify Patricia, a way that would enable him to sleep past eight in the morning without eliciting reproachful lectures on his disregard for her safety. Daniel decided to buy a gun. Marty at the Wampum Store ("Gold and Silver Bought and Sold") offered him a Saturday night special that somebody had traded in for an I.D. bracelet, so Daniel bought the gun and went over to the sheriff's office to apply for a permit. It was a first for Sheriff Duncan Johnson. Most of his constituents owned rifles and shotguns, which did not require permits, and he had never before been required to issue one.

After a futile search for pistol permit forms, Duncan Johnson mulled over the situation and hit upon a solution that seemed to him both simple and practical: he appointed Coltsfoot deputy sheriff. Deputies were entitled to have sidearms without benefit of permit, so Johnson swore him in and sent him about his business. Of course, Daniel did not have a uniform, nor did he participate in any legal functions; it was understood that his appointment was merely a formality designed to foil the bureaucrats in charge of permits. Duncan Johnson would not have dreamed of allowing Dummyweed to patrol the county. The fact that Coltsfoot personified the law on the night of Alex Lerche's murder was pure coincidence—or, as Milo considered it, the malevolence of fate.

Duncan Johnson had gone to the annual North Carolina Sheriffs' Convention, which was being held in Wrightsville Beach. The prospect of ocean fishing had been the main factor in the sheriff's decision to go, but he also hoped to get elected vice-president or perhaps treasurer of the organization. Running for office was a habit with Duncan Johnson. He left the county, peaceful after the early tourist invasion, in the hands of Deputy Pilot Barnes, who had the sense to do what had to be done and leave the rest alone until the boss returned.

Pilot Barnes was doing well in his second day of substitute sheriffing, until 8:00 p.m., when a call came in about a wreck on Whistle Creek, and Pilot had no one to dispatch but himself. He hated to disturb Hamp McKenna, who was his eleven-o'clock replacement. He was debating between calling Hamp and closing the office, when Daniel Hunter Coltsfoot wandered in, asking if he could post a craft fair notice among the wanted posters. Pilot decided that Dummyweed was the least of three evils (by a small margin) and left him in charge of the office, while he went to see about the wreck. After all, he reasoned, Dummyweed was a deputy, and how much trouble could he get into in one hour on a slow night?

*　*　*

It was a wonder he hadn't wrecked the car, Milo thought. His hands were cold with sweat. Despite the shock, though, he thought he had things under control. He was in charge now, and he couldn't worry about the personal side of what had happened. Later, maybe. He was glad he had driven the Sarvice Valley Road so many times. His hands moved the steering wheel at the curves without his conscious thought, and he anticipated the winding of the road, taking it as fast as he dared. He ought to be back in an hour, if they didn't waste too much time at the sheriff's office. He would tell Comfrey Stecoah when they got back, he decided; right now, he wanted to bring in the law.

Milo had left Jake alone at the dig site with the body, and Elizabeth in the church comforting Tessa Lerche and Mary Clare. Or perhaps guarding them. Milo wasn't ready yet to separate mourners from suspects. Victor had turned up in the middle of it all—naturally—and proceeded to dramatize himself by having an asthma attack. Poor Elizabeth. If she could cope with this, she could handle anything.

Milo drove into Laurel Cove, wondering for the first time if he should have come at all. Perhaps he should have telephoned from Sarvice Valley. Surely someone there had a phone; he hadn't thought to ask. They might even tell him that he should have reported this to Bevel Harkness, the Sarvice Valley deputy. Milo frowned. He was damned if he would. Bevel Harkness ranked high on Milo's list of possible murderers, and he intended to tell them that, too. He swung the car into his usual parking place in front of the sheriff's office. He had been in so much wrangling over the computer damage, that he was beginning to feel quite at home there. He wondered if Sheriff Johnson was back from the beach yet, and whether the county's other emergency had come down from the tree of its own accord. The man behind the desk was not Pilot Barnes; after a long look at his outfit, Milo decided that it couldn't possibly be Sheriff Johnson, either. The person on duty was a well-built young man in his mid-twenties, wearing a full-sleeved colonial shirt, burlap trousers, and black moccasins fastened with silver conchos. Milo wondered if this person was a guide who gave tours of "A Backwoods Jail." He glanced about in search of more reliable assistance.

"May I help you?" asked Dummyweed pleasantly.

Milo hesitated. "Are you a deputy?"

"Sure am. Deputy Coltsfoot," he declared, warming to his role. "What's up?"

"I'm here to report a murder."

"Oh, wow!" breathed Coltsfood. "No shit? Who?"

Milo told him.

"Oh, wow!" said Coltsfoot again. "With a *tomahawk?* That's unreal! Well, I'll tell you what to do. Do you drink coffee?"

Milo relaxed a little. "I guess I could use a cup now," he admitted.

"No, man, that's just the point. You've got to cut down on stimulants for the next couple of days—coffee's out of the question. And you ought to increase your intake of vitamins, too. That's to combat stress. Murders are really stressful, man, so you need to watch your metabolism. Got that?"

"Look," said Milo with an edge to his voice, "a man is dead in Sarvice Valley, and I've left him being guarded by a college kid, with a bunch of hysterical possible suspects in the common room of the church. Now where the hell is somebody who knows what to do?"

Coltsfoot sighed. "Pilot *said* he'd be back pretty soon; I guess he'd know what to do."

"Fine. Can you call him?"

"In the patrol car, you mean? I guess so. Do you know how to use the radio there?"

"No," said Milo wearily. "I don't know how to use the radio. Isn't there somebody else we could call?"

Coltsfoot stood up, beaming happily with a new idea. "I tell you what. I'll go along with you to the scene of the crime, so you'll have somebody official there, and I'll leave a note for Pilot on the desk here, and he'll be along when he gets back. Okay?"

Milo nodded. It seemed to be the only thing to do if he wanted to get back anytime soon. He did wonder, though, if Coltsfoot was better than nothing.

Twenty minutes later Pilot Barnes returned to an empty office. He checked the bathroom, and looked into the holding cells in case Dummyweed had decided to grab a nap while he waited, but there was no sign of him. Pilot had just concluded that Dummyweed had got bored and gone home when he saw the note propped on his coffee cup at the front desk. He read the message three times. "Indian Attack in Sarvice Valley," it read. "Man fatally tomahawked. Bring help. (Signed) Deputy D. H. Coltsfoot." Pilot Barnes' first reaction was one of distrust. Indian attack, indeed! "Bring help." The Seventh Cavalry, maybe? He continued to stare at the note, trying to decide that it was a prank so that he could throw it away, but the more he studied it, the more he tended to believe that it was a garbled version of the truth. Pilot could well believe that there had been trouble in Sarvice Valley; the Cullowhees were an ornery bunch of folks, and trouble would be no stranger to that hollow of theirs. It seemed feasible that they had bashed somebody's head in for any number of reasons: poker game, drunk fight, that strip-mining business. He wished Duncan Johnson were back, because he hated to get the coroner out at night on little more than a rumor. He would, though; better safe than sorry.

During the several phone calls that Pilot Barnes made before going out to investigate, he decided to assume an official reticence rather than to admit how little he knew. "Trouble out your way," he told Bevel Harkness. "We're not sure just where. Expect you to find it and report back." He called the chief of the volunteer fire department to borrow the portable generator, in case there was a death scene requiring night lights.

It was more difficult to be evasive with Dr. Putnam, a tiny septuagenarian. "What do you mean, 'trouble in Sarvice Valley,' Pilot Barnes? If you want to get me away from my television, you'll have to do a lot better than that."

"I got a note here that there has been a homicide in Sarvice Valley, and I'd like you to come with me and check it out."

"Can't it wait till morning?" Dr. Putnam insisted. "Some liquored-up Cullowhee probably shot his cousin, and he'll be weeping and wailing over the body by the time you get there. Just bring the body back to town, and I'll do the autopsy first thing in the morning."

"It doesn't sound like that kind of a case," the deputy told him. "My information is that a man was killed with a tomahawk."

"What's that? Did you say tomahawk?"

"According to the information I have," said Pilot Barnes carefully.

"Well, pick me up, boy! I'll even pass up my *Star Trek* rerun for this!"

Half an hour later, one of the volunteer firemen had come in to man the office, and Pilot Barnes was driving out to Sarvice Valley with Deputy Hamp McKenna and Dr. Putnam.

"Wait till Duncan Johnson hears about this!" the old man chuckled. "As soon as he leaves the county, there's an Indian uprising."

"Reckon we ought to notify anybody?" asked Hamp McKenna.

"How about General Custer?" asked Dr. Putnam.

Pilot Barnes, keeping his eyes on the narrow road, was not amused.

On the dark path to the excavation site, Deputy Coltsfoot was feeling considerably less like Gary Cooper in *High Noon*. It had just occurred to him that there was still a murderer at large in the area, and he had not thought to bring a gun with him. He wasn't even sure that he could have found the key to the gun case.

"You don't know who did it, do you?" he asked Milo nervously.

"No. He was dead when I found him. Do you want to take a statement now?"

It was so dark on the path that Coltsfoot couldn't see his own feet, and in any case, he had forgotten to bring a notepad. "I think that can wait awhile," he replied. "You didn't see anybody around, did you?"

"No. Is this your first murder investigation?"

"I guess you could say that," admitted Coltsfoot, neglecting to mention that it was also his first investigation of any kind.

"Well, Dr. Lerche and I work with the coroner's office sometimes back at the university, so I can give you a few pointers if you wouldn't mind."

"Sure. Fire away."

"Well, I think you ought to just stand guard until somebody else gets here," Milo told him. "Don't go looking for footprints, and don't touch anything. The people with the crime kits will want the scene as undisturbed as possible. Your best bet is to secure the area until they get here."

"Secure the area," repeated Coltsfoot, liking the sound of it. "Right." Another thought struck him. "You mean, *by myself?*"

"What kind of an idiot would forget to tell you where the death scene was?" mused Hamp McKenna.

"Dummyweed," grunted Pilot Barnes. "And I was the idiot that left him in charge."

"Drive up to the church," said Dr. Putnam from the back seat. "It's nearly midnight and the lights are on."

When they saw Bevel Harkness' patrol car in the dirt parking lot, they knew they had come to the right place. "Get the camera and the crime kit, Hamp," Pilot ordered, "and follow us up to the church. Those people can tell us where Harkness is."

Dr. Putnam chuckled. "Hope he hasn't gone to join the sheriff's nephew." He meant the one who had disappeared on patrol duty in 1972. "You know, if the Cullowhees have killed an outsider, the wonder of it is that there's a body around to be discovered."

Pilot Barnes sighed. "Bring the rifle too, Hamp."

Inside the church, all was quiet. Victor, whose asthma medicine had finally taken effect, was snoring peacefully in a corner, while the others sipped coffee and talked quietly. To Jake's profound relief, the shock of Lerche's death had stunned Tessa and Mary Clare into numb civility. They sat quietly, speaking in monosyllables, and sipped their coffee as if it were medicine.

Elizabeth was too confused over Dr. Lerche's personal life to feel sympathy for anyone except Milo. Her private opinion of the change in Tessa and Mary Clare was that they both realized the futility of fighting over a dead man. She knew that one of them was going to lose him anyway, and she wondered if that one was secretly pleased that her rival had lost him too. Elizabeth kept these thoughts to herself, dispensing coffee and sympathy as unobtrusively as possible. She wondered when Milo was coming back.

Jake had returned around eleven-thirty, when Milo came back with the deputy. Milo told him to wait at the church for the other officers, while the two of them guarded the site. Jake balanced his coffee mug on his palm and tried to think of something neutral to talk about. He knew Elizabeth wanted to know what was going on up there, but the presence of two mourners prevented them from discussing it.

"He never got to finish his project," Tessa murmured.

"The discriminate function chart?" asked Elizabeth.

"Yes. It was nearly ready, and he was so excited about it. It would have been such a contribution to the field." Tears streamed down her cheeks. "And he never got to use the riding lawn mower, either!"

"What's going to become of the project?" asked Elizabeth.

"I think we ought to finish it," said Mary Clare.

"Yeah, me too," mumbled Jake. "Sort of a memorial."

"But, how can we? I mean, do we have the expertise?" Elizabeth protested.

Jake shrugged. "Let's talk it over with Milo. He may have some ideas on that." He sat up. "Was that headlights in the parking lot? I think the sheriff has arrived."

Pilot Barnes peered past Jake into the common room. "Is this where the homicide is?" he demanded.

"Yes. I mean—no. The body is up at the dig site. Your deputies are up there with one of our people, and they told me to show you the way."

Dr. Putnam cocked his head and looked appraisingly at Jake. "You're not a Cullowhee, are you, boy?"

Jake blinked. "No, sir."

"What's your last name?"

"Adair."

The doctor nodded, satisfied. "Ah! So that's it!" He turned and followed the procession up the trail to the cemetery.

Pilot Barnes spent most of the walk barking questions at Jake, beginning with: "Ain't you the people whose computer got smashed?"

Jake said that they were, and Pilot digested this information for several minutes, trying to connect it with the homicide. "But you didn't have a computer up there at the cemetery, did you?"

"No."

"Did you have any trouble with the Cullowhees? That's their kin you're digging up, you know."

"They asked us to come," said Jake. He explained the purpose of the dig.

Pilot Barnes frowned. This wasn't going to be like their usual brand of homicide, which took all of about twenty minutes to solve. This one felt like a needle in a tub of molasses. He wondered how Duncan Johnson managed to be away when it happened: second sight or undeserved good luck? Pilot decided that he would do the essential site investigation tonight—he could hardly do otherwise—but that to continue the case without notifying his superior would be overstepping his authority. Beach or no beach, Duncan Johnson was getting a phone call in the morning.

They threaded their way past empty graves to the tent. In the lantern light, Pilot could see Bevel Harkness and Dummyweed talking to the young man who had come in to report the computer damage.

"It's just that Indian curse I was a-telling you 'bout," Harkness was saying in sepulchral tones. "They went and got him for sacrilege."

"Harkness, that's not how we expect officers to talk while investigating a homicide," growled Pilot Barnes. He did not like Harkness at the best of times, and his opinion had scarcely altered with what he had just heard. He turned to the other of his least favorite people. "Coltsfoot, that note you left me wasn't exactly a wealth of information."

He took the criticism philosophically. "It was hard

to know what to say. I was pretty reamed out myself by the news, you know?"

"Just remember to tell *where* as well as *what.*" Pilot turned to Hamp McKenna. "I think you can put that generator on the edge of the clearing so the light shines this way. Is the body in there?"

Milo, to whom the question was addressed, opened the tent flap and ushered the deputy in. Pilot Barnes took in the scene with considerably less emotion than that displayed by Coltsfoot. He stared at the body for several minutes without speaking.

"What are you going to do now?" asked Milo softly.

"Usual procedure," said Pilot, still staring at the body. "Photographs, site investigation. Dr. Putnam out there is the coroner, and he'll do an examination in situ. We'll secure the area until sunup; ought to be able to tell more then."

Milo hesitated. "Well, that's what I wanted to ask about, really. Who are you planning to leave guarding the scene?"

Sensing that there might be a logical reason for the question, Pilot replied: "Bevel Harkness, I reckon. We're shorthanded."

"Uh ... I don't mean to tell you your job, but I don't think that's a very good idea, since this is a murder."

"Oh? And why not?"

In a low voice, Milo told him about Harkness's appearance at the Cullowhees' meeting, and about his warnings of "Indian curses" should the project continue. "I don't think he'd be the most objective of investigators, Mr. Barnes," Milo concluded.

Pilot Barnes nodded. He wouldn't have to wait for Duncan's okay on this one; they were of the same mind about Harkness. "I take your meaning," he said to Milo. He went back outside, motioning for Dr. Putnam to take over.

"McKenna, how's your work coming?"

The deputy looked up from his camera. "As well as could be expected," he said. "We'll know more in the morning."

"All right. McKenna, I want you to finish up here, and get these pictures developed, and relieve Harvey Jeffers at the office. He's sitting in for us right now. Coltsfoot, you're going to start earning your keep as a deputy of this county. I'm putting you on guard duty here to secure the area—*only* because we're shorthanded. We'll be back in the morning to relieve you."

"What about me?" Harkness demanded.

"I hear you have some opinions about this stripmining business."

"Damn right I do. I don't want this land to be roped off by the federal government like some kind of a people zoo, so—"

"Well, be that as it may, in a murder investigation it's a conflict of interest, and I'm taking you off the case. You can continue your regular patrols in the valley until further notice, but you are to have nothing to do with this homicide investigation. You got that?"

"I got it, all right," muttered Harkness, turning to go.

"You want me to stay here all night?" gasped Coltsfoot. "Is *he* still gonna be here?" He gestured toward the tent.

"No. After McKenna takes his photos, we'll take him on back to town for the autopsy," said Pilot.

"Well, what about all those skulls in there?"

"They stay here," said Milo promptly. "They have no bearing on the case, and we need them to continue the project."

"Oh, you're going on with it, are you?" asked Pilot Barnes.

"Oh, yes," said Milo softly. "I'm going on with it."

"Well, are any of those people planning to leave the area? I need to get statements from everybody, but it can be left till the morning if they'll all be around."

"Well ... there's two of them I'm not sure about. Dr. Lerche's wife ... widow."

"Oh, Lord! The widow is here?"

"Arrived tonight. I expect she will go back to the university to make arrangements for the funeral and so forth. She may want to speak to you now, so that she can leave in the morning."

"Who's the other one?"

Milo hesitated. "Dr. Lerche's graduate assistant, Mary Clare Gitlin. She was supposed to go off and do research, I think. I haven't had much time to talk to the group tonight."

"Come on, I'll walk back to the church with you," Barnes offered. "You look like you're on your last legs. Just let me tell the doc to meet us there when he's through."

Milo wished he had brought a jacket. Mountain nights were chilly, even in late summer. He was glad of the cold, though, because it kept him awake despite his tiredness. He hoped that the numbness of fatigue, which was hitting his legs and his shoulders, would seep into his brain sooner or later and allow him to sleep. He didn't want to face what was left of the night staring into the darkness seeing Alex face-down among the Indian skulls.

"I reckon I ought to get preliminary statements from everybody tonight," Pilot Barnes remarked. "While it's still fresh in their minds."

Milo shrugged. "Why not? I doubt if they'll be asleep yet."

"Why don't we start with you, to pass the time while we're walking? You found the body, didn't you?"

"Yes. I had just come back from Laurel Cove, from setting up the new monitor in the motel room. Mrs. Lerche had just arrived, and she asked me to take

113

her up to the site, where Alex was working. Apparently he wanted to see me about something, too."

"Oh? What about?" Pilot's voice had lost its casual tone.

"I don't know; he was dead when I got there. I don't think it had any bearing on this, though. It was probably something about the project. A measurement he wanted taken, or some data looked up."

Pilot shrugged. That seemed logical to him, too. "Why would somebody have wanted to kill this fellow?" he asked.

"I don't think it was personal," said Milo. "I think somebody wanted the strip-mining company to get the land, and that they killed Alex because he might have proved the Indians' claim, which would give them the land."

"Somebody who favored the strip miners," mused Pilot. "Such as Bevel Harkness?"

"He's on the top of my list," said Milo.

Pilot Barnes looked around the Sunday school room at the sleeping bags and cooking utensils. His eyes came to rest on Victor, snoring peacefully against the wall.

"Is there someplace private I can go to talk to folks?" he asked in a pained voice.

"How about the sanctuary?" asked Jake.

Pilot thought this over for a few moments, without being able to come up with a better idea. "Well," he said at last, "it might encourage them to tell me the truth."

Pilot thought it looked like an ordinary little country church—seating capacity maybe seventy-five, too poor for stained glass, upright piano, and varnished pine pulpit in front of homemade velvet curtains, which concealed nothing but a whitewashed wall. No holy of holies here. He'd wondered if the Cullowhees

114

were footwashers or snake handlers, but seeing the sanctuary he reckoned not.

He ushered Mrs. Lerche gently to the front pew and pulled up the piano bench for himself. "Now, ma'am, I know it's awful to be put through this in your time of sorrow, but you must understand that I have to do it."

Tessa nodded. "I won't be much help," she said in a voice of quiet composure. "I just got here, and I'm afraid I know very little about the project." In the same unemotional tone, she gave him a sketch of her day, ending when Milo had come out of the tent and led her back to the church, telling her that Alex was dead. "It seems very strange that he should be dead," she said in a puzzled voice.

"I expect it does, ma'am," said Pilot politely. "Do you have any idea as to who would want to kill him?"

Tessa turned to him wide-eyed. "Why, no. Not if some local person did it. They might perhaps have misunderstood about his work."

The deputy sensed that he was being invited to pursue the matter. He obliged. "And if it *wasn't* a local?"

"I did think that perhaps Mary Clare . . . ," Tessa murmured, twisting her rings.

"Mary Clare? The graduate assistant?"

"Oh, I'm sure it's nothing to interest you, Sheriff," said Tessa with a gentle smile. "It's just that the poor thing had sort of a schoolgirl crush on my husband, as students will often do."

There had to be more to it than that. Pilot waited.

"And I think she misunderstood my husband's . . . encouragement of her work. I'm afraid she became rather silly about it, and he was forced to hurt her feelings. It was all very embarrassing for him."

Pilot grunted. He had waded through all the flowers in Tessa's explanation, and had concluded that the professor was fooling around with his assistant. In his book, that made two suspects with good

115

motives: the girlfriend and the wife. "I'll look into it," he said noncommittally.

"I'm sure it's nothing," murmured Tessa, but she sounded pleased.

Pilot decided that at this point Duncan Johnson would interview someone besides the girlfriend. That way he could have a little hearsay to contribute to the conversation. People often said more when they had something to refute. He could have chosen any of the others to question next; the fact that he picked Victor was sheer spite. The sight of him snoring like a hog through a murder investigation made Pilot Barnes long to kick him; he settled for a rude awakening and some less-than-polite questioning.

"*I* don't know who killed him," Victor sulked. "He wasn't a very nice man."

"Wasn't he?" asked Pilot genially.

Victor, detecting a sympathetic listener, told his version of the Peking man incident. In revised form, Victor was now convinced that he had made a slip of the tongue in a technical matter, and that Lerche had chosen to misinterpret his mistake, and to publicly humiliate him for it.

The deputy was puzzled. "What does it matter which pile of bones you saw in the museum?" he asked.

Victor smiled bitterly. "I assure you that anthropologists are perfectly capable of pitching fits over matters even more trivial than that."

"Well, did he put anybody else's back up thataway?"

"Not that I recall," said Victor, implying that he had a mind above such things.

"There's always his personal life to consider," said Pilot carefully. "That business about his graduate student."

"*Wasn't* it awful?" Victor nodded. "I wasn't here

116

when The Wife showed up, but I imagine that it was quite a scene. Elizabeth and Jake seemed most uncomfortable."

"Oh, you were out?"

"Yes. After that dreadful incident with Dr. Lerche, I had the most piercing migraine. The very air seemed to oppress me. Naturally, I went outside for a while in an attempt to lessen the agony. It's merciful I wasn't present for that scene between Mrs. Lerche and Mary Clare, because it would have been very bad for my nerves."

"How do you know there was a scene between them if you weren't around?" asked Pilot.

"When I came back in—",

"What time was that?"

Victor looked pained. "One doesn't clock-watch on a dig. Nine-thirty or so, I expect. Well past dark. Anyway, when I came in, there was a strained atmosphere, as if everyone had just been at each other's throats."

"What were you doing wandering around in the dark till nine-thirty?" Pilot made the question an expression of friendly interest rather than an accusation.

"It's obvious that you've never had a migraine," said Victor with dark satisfaction. "Light hurts one's eyes. I was just walking about in the dark waiting for the pounding to subside. Of course, I would have been better off lying down, but they were not going to turn off the lights in the common room. No one has any concern for my feelings."

"Did you happen to go up to the cemetery?"

Victor hesitated. "Well ... perhaps in that direction," he admitted. "But I didn't see anything."

"How close did you get?"

"I may have just glimpsed the tent light shining through the trees. I didn't see any movement."

"Was that when you just started out or just before you came back in?"

"Somewhere in the middle, I guess."

Pilot Barnes sighed. Any hope of fixing the time of death had better not be pinned on this tomfool witness. He thanked him, and sent for Mary Clare.

Mary Clare did not wait to be questioned. "Have you made an arrest yet?" she demanded.

Pilot Barnes blinked. "You have anybody in mind?"

"There's some idiot loose in these hills bashing people on the head, buddy, and you'd better find him."

"You oughtn't to let it frighten you," said Pilot soothingly.

"Frighten me? I wish they'd tried to get me instead of Alex! I'd have left 'em laying on the ground!" Her voice softened. "I don't think Alex was much of a fighter. I wish I'da walked that way tonight."

"Walked that way? Were you out tonight?"

"I went for a walk. Why?"

Pilot grimaced. "Seems like the whole world was out walking the woods tonight."

"Oh," said Mary Clare, suddenly comprehending. "You're thinking about alibis."

"Have to."

"Well, I didn't kill Alex. Had no reason to."

"I understand there was a little misunderstanding between the two of you. Something about a schoolgirl crush."

He expected to get a rise out of her with that phrase, but she recognized the wording as Tessa's, and only said: "I told you Alex wasn't much of a fighter."

Pilot continued with a few routine questions about where Mary Clare was and when, but the emotional outburst he was hoping for didn't come.

"Will I be able to leave?" Mary Clare asked when he had finished.

"Where were you planning to go?"

"Alex asked me to go and do some research at MacDowell College, and I'd like to follow through on it. This project was important to him."

Pilot nodded. "That's within the state. I don't see why not. Just let us know where you can be reached in case we need you."

"I'll be back," said Mary Clare.

"Adair. A-D-A-I-R," said Jake.

"And what is your position?"

"I'm an undergrad, which means that I do the pick-and-shovel work in exchange for the experience."

"Did you get along with Dr. Lerche?"

"Oh, sure. I didn't have much to do with him, anyway. Mary Clare was the site manager."

"And where were you tonight?"

"From supper on, I was in the church, trying to read a book."

"So you didn't go out in the woods?"

"No. Not until Milo found the body and sent me up there to guard it. I didn't see or hear anyone around then."

"I bet you saw and heard a lot at the church, though," said Pilot slyly. "About the time Mrs. Lerche arrived and met the girlfriend."

Jake shrugged. "There wasn't much to it."

"Don't you find it odd that the site manager is being sent off to do research someplace else?"

"Not if that's what needed doing," Jake replied calmly. "Milo could site-manage. I could do it myself."

"Do you have any opinions on who would go after your boss with a tomahawk?"

"Oh, sure. Some local in favor of the strip-mining deal who wanted to make the Cullowhees look bad. I see racial overtones, don't you?"

Pilot Barnes shook his head. "I see a long case," he

sighed, "with the sheriff gone, and me supposed to put up hay tomorrow. Why me, Lord?"

"Are you sure he was murdered?" asked Elizabeth, wide-eyed.

"Yes, ma'am," said Pilot patiently. "People don't generally sneak up and hit themselves on the back of the head with a tomahawk."

"I guess not." She nodded. "By the way, do you know Wesley Rountree?"

This was a name none of the others had mentioned. A new lead, thought Pilot. "Is he one of the people connected with this project?" he asked.

"Oh, no. He's the sheriff of Chandler Grove, Georgia, where my cousins live. I just thought you might know him, since you're in law enforcement too."

"No, ma'am," said the deputy, forgoing the desire to tell her that he was not acquainted with Wyatt Earp or Buford Pusser either. "Now could you give me a statement about what happened tonight?"

Elizabeth told him about her evening, describing the encounter between Mary Clare and Tessa Lerche as tactfully as she could. She had not left the church since supper, she said, and she had no information relevant to the incident.

"Actually, I'm not an anthropologist," she admitted. "I came on this dig because I thought it sounded interesting."

"Who invited you?"

"Um . . . Milo Gordon. He's my brother's roommate, and . . ."

"I see," said Pilot Barnes. And he did.

The next morning at nine, Dr. Putnam found Pilot Barnes going through a pile of papers on Duncan Johnson's desk. He halted his search periodically to take gulps of coffee from a mug on the top of the filing cabinet.

"What did you lose?" asked Dr. Putnam. "Not evidence, I hope."

"Nope. I'm hunting the address of that sheriff's convention at the beach."

"I thought you'd be wanting to wash your hands of this case, Pilot."

The deputy shrugged. A certain kind of person always made that joke sooner or later. He said, "I just think he ought to be told. If he still wants me to handle it, that's fine."

"Well, I figured you'd want to get in touch with him, so I hurried through your autopsy first thing. Can't sleep of a morning anyway anymore."

"What did you find?"

"Oh, it was just what it looked like. Somebody bashed his head in with that ridiculous tomahawk, and that's exactly what killed him. I'll give you a typed-up version in two-dollar words this afternoon. This one doesn't need to go to the state lab, though, so you go right on ahead with the investigation. Did the tomahawk tell you anything?"

"The handle was rough bark, which doesn't take fingerprints. There was a paper seal on the bottom saying Made in Taiwan. They sell them at Cherokee for four bucks."

Dr. Putnam shook his head. "All I can say is, when it comes my time to go, I hope I don't die in a *silly* way." He snorted. "Dyed chicken feathers and plastic string!"

Pilot Barnes, who had found the number of the sheriff's hotel and was busy dialing it, did not reply. Dr. Putnam had nothing further to report on the Lerche case, but he wouldn't have missed the forthcoming conversation for the world. He settled down in the straight chair and began to leaf through Duncan Johnson's current copy of *Field and Stream*.

"Official police call for Sheriff Duncan Johnson,"

said Pilot Barnes in his most matter-of-fact tone. He drummed his fingers on the desk while he waited for the harassed receptionist to sort through one hundred sheriffs' messages for the whereabouts of Sheriff Johnson. "Yeah. I'm still here. He—what? Okay. When do you think that'll be? Well, ask him to call his office." He hung up the phone with more force than necessary.

Dr. Putnam, who was helping himself to coffee, raised his eyebrows expectantly.

The deputy scowled. "He went deep-sea fishing with the guys from Buncombe County. They're staying overnight on the boat."

The doctor's eyes twinkled. "Call out the Coast Guard! Boy, wouldn't I love to see Duncan Johnson's face when the floating feds hauled him off that fishing boat."

Pilot Barnes, who had been thinking of doing just that, did not smile. "I guess it's up to me, then," he said, but he wrote the phone number of Duncan Johnson's hotel on the front of the phone book.

CHAPTER NINE

MILO WATCHED it grow light. Across the valley the intersecting planes of woods and pasture changed from gray to green against the black shapes of the mountains. He had grown tired of fighting for sleep at five in the morning and slipped out of the church. He filled the bucket at the nearby stream so that he could start the coffee before the others woke up. Alex used to get up early too, Milo thought. Many mornings he would come into the office straight from a hot shower in the gym, following his morning run. He used to ask Milo to join him, but Milo never took him up on it. He would always answer that during his career as all-night security person he had seen enough sunrises to last him a lifetime. He wasn't awake now to appreciate the beauty of the morning.

"Milo?" Elizabeth peered out of the side door of the church, yawning sleepily. "What time is it?"

"Quarter past dawn," said Milo absently.

"How long have you been out here?"

"I don't know. I thought I'd make coffee as long as I was up."

"Is it ready? The deputy up at the site might like some."

Milo looked down at the bucket of water beside him. "I forgot to make it."

Elizabeth sighed. "Wait here."

In a few minutes she had returned with the camp stove, the large yellow coffee funnel, and a pot to boil the water in. Scooping water from the bucket into the pot, Elizabeth said, "I'll brew it up out here. That

123

way I won't wake up anyone inside, and you won't be alone."

"I don't feel like talking," said Milo.

"Very likely not," nodded Elizabeth. "But why don't you think out loud?"

"I just can't believe Alex is dead," said Milo. "To Alex death wasn't an inevitability, it was a puzzle."

"How so?" asked Elizabeth quietly as she spooned coffee into the filter.

"A corpse was a puzzle. What could it tell us by this bruise or that distortion of bones? I guess I always thought of Alex as manipulating death . . . to make it tell us things. Now he's just another case for some other examiner. An occipital fracture to be catalogued with the rest."

"Not to you. He'll never be just another case to you. The question is: where do we go from here?"

Milo, startled out of his reverie, looked at her for the first time. "What do you mean?"

"The project. Do we pack it in, or what? The others will be wanting to know."

Milo was looking toward the path that led to the excavation site. The woods were still dark, so that the path seemed to be a strip of light that stopped abruptly at the trees.

"You realize, of course, that there is a murderer out there, and he could be waiting to pick off the rest of us?" Elizabeth shivered.

"Of course I realize it! Why else would I be hesitating about finishing the project? I want to do this as a memorial to Alex—but I can't let his students get killed in the process."

"I'm going inside to get the cups," said Elizabeth.

When she came back, Milo had not moved. He was still staring out across the valley, lost in thought. Elizabeth poured the coffee. "You know, Alex's death may not have anything to do with the project," she remarked, trying to sound casual.

Milo grunted. "What about the computer damage? Was that a coincidence too?"

"I guess not," Elizabeth admitted. "I wish I knew what Alex wanted to talk to you about."

Milo looked up. "What do you mean?"

"Before you got back from town last night, he came into the church looking for you. I got the impression that he wanted to ask you something."

"What else did he say?"

"Just that you should go up to the site when you came in. Oh, and before that he told me that he had checked my skull measurements."

"How were they?"

"He didn't say. What do you suppose that means?"

"I don't know. Maybe nothing, but it's all we have to go on. I'm going to check those skulls."

"So we're going on with the project?"

Milo poured his untasted coffee into the weeds. "I am, anyway."

Milo waited until after breakfast to talk to the group. Not that a discussion of business would have dampened the meal; hardly a word was spoken. Still, he wanted their full attention when he spoke, because he was conscious of the formality of the occasion. They were all looking at him with the embarrassment caused by the presence of unshared grief. He wondered if Mary Clare had recovered from her infatuation, or if she was trying to avoid pity.

"I think we should talk about what we're going to do," Milo began uncertainly. "I guess all of you realize that Alex Lerche was a dedicated scientist who was about to make a great contribution to anthropology when he . . . when he died," Milo finished faintly.

"And Milo wants us to carry on with the project," said Elizabeth quickly, before he could get wound up again.

"Of course he does," said Mary Clare.

"But the man was murdered!" sputtered Victor. "Surely we can't stay up here in the woods with a killer loose!"

"Maybe we ought to vote on it," said Milo.

Jake stood up. "It is for us, the living, rather to be dedicated here to the unfinished work they have thus far so nobly advanced," he said solemnly.

"Damn straight," said Mary Clare. "Y'all can vote all you want. Alex told me to do research at Mac-Dowell, and I'm going."

"Jake, that was a beautiful speech," whispered Elizabeth when he sat down.

"Yep." nodded Jake. "Gettysburg Address. It seemed appropriate."

"I'm going to stay," said Milo. "And since I'll be heading up this project, maybe I'll be in the most danger, but I think I owe it to Alex to finish. Anyone who wants to stay with me is welcome." He looked doubtfully at Elizabeth. "Maybe you ought to check with your folks or something, though."

Elizabeth was indignant. "I'm a college graduate too, you know! Just because you live with my big brother doesn't mean you have to act like him! Of course I'm staying!" She had not considered the question at all, but Milo's protective attitude had settled it.

"I'm staying too," said Jake.

Victor signed. "I suppose I shall carry on," he said grudgingly. "I know how much Dr. Lerche relied on me."

Mary Clare stifled a giggle. "Well," she said. "I'm all packed, so I reckon I ought to get on the road."

Elizabeth frowned. "What about the funeral?" she asked. "Shouldn't we go to that?"

"No," said Mary Clare. "That funeral is going to be a faculty meeting run by the well-dressed widow. If you want to remember Alex, you'd best do it right here."

"I'd like to go," said Milo softly, "but I think if it were up to Alex, he'd want us right here."

"It's settled then," said Jake. "We carry on."

Daniel Hunter Coltsfoot accepted the thermos of coffee as if he were a prisoner instead of a deputy. He had passed an uneasy night among the skulls in the site tent, listening intently for mountain lions and ax murderers—neither of which had disturbed his night-long vigil. Elizabeth and Milo had taken the precaution of hailing him from the edge of the clearing, in case he had been provided with a loaded gun for the occasion. When he peered out of the tent at them, Elizabeth waved the thermos and called out, "Good morning!"

Coltsfoot hurried out of the tent, remembered the possible presence of evidence, and began to tiptoe toward them like one crossing a minefield. "Boy, am I glad to see you guys!" he announced. "Is that for me? Wow, thanks. You think it's okay to drink on the job?"

"As long as it's coffee," Milo assured him with a straight face.

"Thanks. Have you seen Pilot Barnes this morning?"

"I expect he'll be along," said Milo. "We wanted to get back to work."

"Oh, gee, I don't know about that," said Coltsfoot. "They said something about coming back this morning to check for evidence."

"It's okay. We won't disturb the site until they've been over it. But they took pictures in the tent last night, didn't they?"

Coltsfoot tried to remember. "I think so."

"All we want are the skulls from inside the tent," Elizabeth said. "I want to remeasure them. I expect you'll be glad to have them out of the way, won't you?"

Coltsfoot frowned, suspecting a slight on his bravery. "It's all in the line of duty, ma'am," he drawled.

"I'm sure it is," said Elizabeth quickly. "I only meant that an outdoor man like yourself must feel cramped in that tiny tent, and we could get that box out of your way."

"We'd be right where you could see us," Milo put in. "Just under that tree over there, doing measurements. You can watch."

"I don't know . . ." Coltsfoot struck a pose, pretending to conjure up the regulations he had never seen.

"We'd like to go on with our work . . . as therapy for our grief," said Elizabeth with a soulful look into the deputy's eyes.

"Well, gee . . . I can relate to that. Okay, pack 'em up. I don't see what harm it could do since the body's gone."

"I don't see what those skull measurements have to do with Alex's death," Elizabeth whispered when they were out of earshot.

"Just a hunch," murmured Milo, turning a skull upside down. "Did you have to say that bit about therapy for our grief?"

"I'm sorry, Milo. But it worked. It got you the skulls. Now what are you looking for?"

"Never mind," said Milo, intent on his examination.

"You don't think *I* killed him for criticizing my work?"

"Shhh! Keep your voice down. Anyway, he didn't criticize your work, did he?"

"No," Elizabeth admitted. "But you have only my word for that. Anyway, I'd be surprised if I did everything exactly right. I *am* new at it."

"I don't think that's what Alex wanted to see me about," Milo whispered. "He would have understood all that. Besides, I'm not checking measurements."

Elizabeth looked at the way he was handling the skull, noticing for the first time that he had not picked up a measuring tool at all. "No, you aren't," she agreed. "What *are* you doing?"

Milo glanced furtively in the direction of the tent, but Coltsfoot was not watching them. "I'm looking for a ringer."

"I beg your pardon?"

"A ringer. Now, you can't mention this to anybody. Do you understand that? Especially not the sheriff's department."

"I promise, Milo."

"All right. Don't react when I tell you this. I think one of those skulls isn't what it's supposed to be. Alex must have noticed it."

"You mean one is a fake? I know I'm a beginner, but I certainly would have noticed that!" said Elizabeth indignantly.

Milo sighed. "I don't mean a plastic one, Elizabeth. Of course they're all real skulls; but they are all supposed to belong to early nineteenth-century Indians. Now suppose one of them isn't."

"Isn't a nineteenth-century Indian?"

"Right. What better way to dispose of a murder victim than to bury him with a bunch of other bodies?"

Elizabeth nodded. "Can you prove it?"

"More than likely—if I'm right."

"How?"

"Lots of ways. Depends on how long it has been buried. If it has been there less than five years, the skull should be lighter than the rest. Of course, the easy way to tell—if we get lucky—is the teeth."

"Of course! If the ringer has metal tooth fillings in his mouth, we can be pretty sure he wasn't a nine-teenth-century Indian." Elizabeth picked up a battered brown skull and peered at the dark stumps on the maxilla. "This one definitely never saw a dentist," she announced.

Milo tapped the smooth cranium. "It was pretty old. No suture closures."

They worked for a while in silence, comparing skull coloration, and brushing dirt away from molars to see if a dark filling lay concealed beneath. Occasionally Milo would pick up a measuring tool if Coltsfoot happened to be looking in their direction.

"Why don't you want the sheriff's men to know what you suspect?" asked Elizabeth after a while.

"Because if a new body was dumped into the gravesite, it was done by the locals. We're outsiders. I don't know who we can trust."

"Suddenly I don't feel very safe," said Elizabeth. She looked at Coltsfoot out of the corner of her eye, wondering if he was as innocuous as he appeared.

"I just wish I knew who we're looking for," said Milo fiercely. "That would help. I wonder if there is any way that we could discreetly ask questions about missing persons around the area."

Elizabeth's eyes widened. "Missing persons! Milo! I think I know who we're looking for."

In an urgent undertone she recounted the details of the Moonshine Massacre, ending with the disappearance of the sheriff's nephew. "And he has not been found to this day," she finished solemnly.

Milo rocked back on his heels and picked up a skull from the box. "That must be it," he agreed. "One of these skulls must be him." After a moment's scrutiny, he set the skull back in the box. "Not this one, though. Keep looking."

He watched for a moment as Elizabeth deftly hoisted another specimen. She had a steady hand, without a trace of beginner's squeamishness. "You're doing very well, Elizabeth," he said awkwardly. "I'd just like you to know that—"

Elizabeth shook her head. "No, Milo," she said gently. "Not until this is over."

Pilot Barnes and Hamp McKenna rode in silence along the Sarvice Valley Road. Pilot was too preoccupied with his newly complicated responsibilities to engage in small talk, but despite his worries, he looked out across the valley with a stir of satisfaction. There were pastures of scrubby black cattle, and mounds of green hills attached like ribs to the spine of a wooded mountain. Weathered barns and laden apple trees became postcard pictures framed by split-rail fences.

At least this hasn't changed, Pilot thought. He wished he could say the same for the rest of the county. The new four-lane, which had been built to speed tourists on their way to Asheville, and the motels and gift shops designed to slow them down, were sources of jobs and revenue, he supposed, but their ugliness saddened him. A mainstream of American culture had washed over the mountains, drowning most of what had been there before, and leaving flotsam of rusted car bodies and old beer cans. Pilot Barnes wondered how long the Cullowhees could hold out against the tide, or if in fact they wanted to.

"Wonder how Dummyweed passed the night," Hamp mused, an edge of sarcasm in his voice.

Pilot grunted. Assigning Dummyweed to guard duty had started him on this train of thought, he guessed, because Dummyweed was a perfect example of the county's new settlers. They arrived in minivans, armed with *Foxfire* books to teach them how to live "country," and they built forty-thousand-dollar log homes with solar water heaters. He saw them as year-round tourists, who sold their pots and dulcimers to the more seasonal variety. And now, with Duncan Johnson gone ocean-fishing, the county had its first instance of computer crime and complicated homicide. He might have known it would come to this. Pilot Barnes felt a little like an Indian watching the wagon trains roll toward his hunting grounds.

* * *

In daylight the clearing seemed less ominous, Pilot thought, threading his way past the trenches. In June, when the mountain laurel bushes were blooming, it was probably beautiful. Pilot thought cemeteries ought to be beautiful; he didn't hold with making horrors out of people just because they had died.

"Good morning," said Dummyweed with more than a trace of eagerness in his voice. "Everything's fine here."

Pilot edged past him and peered into the tent. "It is, huh?" he barked. "Then suppose you tell me where the contents of that tent went to!"

Daniel Hunter Coltsfoot paled. "Contents?"

"When we took the body out of here last night, there were skulls all over the place in there. Where are they?"

"Over there! They said they needed them to do their research. They said that they weren't important to the case. They said—"

Pilot cut him off with a nod. "I'll handle it. You go on home now." You couldn't fire someone who wasn't on the payroll, the deputy reasoned. He motioned for Hamp to begin the routine investigation.

Elizabeth and Milo, having seen the uniformed deputies approach, were busy with their measuring instruments, apparently oblivious to the new arrivals. When Pilot Barnes loomed over them, blocking their light, they looked up in all innocence. "Good morning," said Elizabeth politely.

Pilot Barnes' lips tightened. "Tampering with evidence in a homicide constitutes being an accessory after the fact," he informed them.

Milo sighed. "Look, I've worked on cases with our coroner back home. Why don't you call him? His name is Dr. David—"

"Makes no difference," said the deputy, shaking his head. "Everybody here is a suspect until I know

132

different from my own investigations. I'm going to impound those skulls as material evidence."

"Evidence of what?" Milo demanded.

Pilot gave him an appraising stare. "I'll bet you could tell me that."

"The deputy won't let us work up there today," Milo told the assembled diggers. "I'm sorry we couldn't let you guys know before you drove all the way up here."

"That's okay," said the president of the archaeological society. "We're sorry to hear about Dr. Lerche. What happens now?"

"We've decided to continue. I'm going to town this afternoon and call the chairman of the anthropology department. I'm pretty sure he'll let me finish the project on my own. It's only a couple of weeks. Come back tomorrow. We'll be back in business by then."

When the local workers had gone back to their cars, Milo turned to Jake. "I need to go to town to make phone calls. You're in charge while I'm gone. Don't let the sheriff's department impound our equipment or anything, but otherwise, cooperate with them."

Jake nodded. "Anything you want us to do?"

"No. Just stay out of trouble."

"Do the police have any leads on the killer?" asked Victor, lapsing into television cop talk.

Milo gave him a grim smile. "We seem to be their first choice," he said.

"Have you told Comfrey Stecoah about this, Milo?" asked Elizabeth.

"I expect he knows. But you're right. He ought to hear it from me. I'll stop by this afternoon."

"Milo, would you like me to come with you?" asked Elizabeth. She tried frantically to think of some grocery item they might need, which could only be chosen by herself. No inspiration was forthcoming.

"No, thanks," said Milo. "I need the time."

When he had gone, Elizabeth turned to Jake. "I hope they solve it soon, Jake. Milo looks awful!"

Jake nodded. "He's going to have to eat one of these days."

Victor nodded. "It's dreadful. I have had to force myself to eat. I simply will not give way to nerves! But I really don't see why this case is dragging on. It is perfectly obvious who the killer is."

"It isn't obvious to me," Elizabeth told him.

He smiled complacently. "Ah! Perhaps you don't see things as I do!"

CHAPTER TEN

ELIZABETH, preoccupied with thoughts of the murder and its aftermath, did not stop to look at the plants along the trail. She might have noticed a coiled snake or a clump of poison oak, if her foot had been about to land on either, but otherwise she was oblivious to her surroundings. Not the right frame of mind in which to visit the Wise Woman of the Woods, she thought, but she was going anyway. When she mentioned to Milo that someone should tell Comfrey about Alex, it had suddenly occurred to her that Amelanchier was an elderly woman living alone in the woods. She should know about the danger. Elizabeth decided that she would feel better knowing that Amelanchier was all right; and perhaps the Wise Woman would have some bit of advice to comfort her.

Amelanchier was outside her cabin, talking to some visitors. Not wanting to interrupt, Elizabeth stayed hidden in a clump of laurels and listened to the consultation.

"Don't forget what I told you about drinking sassafras tea," Amelanchier was saying to a tall woman wearing a sundress. "Beets and asparagus'll do you good too."

The woman was nodding, absorbed in the lecture, while her husband, a red-faced man in doubleknit trousers and a pink polo shirt, was circling the two of them with his camera. "Ann, move your shoulder a little to the right," he commanded. "The light's not right."

Amelanchier looked him over carefully and turned

back to the woman. "Now, you mind what I told you about brewing your bitters from them herbs I give you."

"Yes. Yes. I've written it down," the woman assured her.

"All right," said Amelanchier doubtfully. "But don't you use no city water, and don't cook it up in no aluminum pan, neither."

"Copper?" asked the woman anxiously.

Amelanchier was scornful. "Copper's for moonshine," she declared. "You want to use enamel or stainless steel."

"I will! I will!" the woman promised.

"How much do we owe you?" asked the man, lowering his camera.

"You got four bags of bitters, and two gallon jugs of it already made up. That'll be seven dollars."

The man smiled. "Do you have change for a twenty?"

Amelanchier hesitated. "Take it on," she said, waving him away. "You can pay me when you've got it."

The woman started to protest, but her husband led her down the path, smirking at having got something for nothing.

Elizabeth glared at them from the laurel bush. They acted as if Amelanchier were an exhibit in a zoo, she thought angrily. "Why did you let that awful man get away with that?" she demanded, marching out from her hiding place.

Amelanchier shook her head. "I didn't hardly like to charge her. She was buying the medicine for him, and you could see he wasn't going to take it."

"What was the matter with him?" asked Elizabeth. He had seemed healthy enough.

"Did you look at his hands? That's the best way to tell." She shook her head, dismissing the tourist couple from her thoughts. She turned back to Elizabeth with a happy smile. "You're looking a little peaky yourself, gal. What's been going on down there?"

Elizabeth told her, omitting only the details of Alex's personal problems with his wife and Mary Clare. "I came up to see if you were all right," she added.

"Shoot far," snorted Amelanchier, easing herself onto a wooden bench on the porch. "I've lived by myself in these woods for a coon's age. Don't you worry about me. But I'm sorry to hear about your boss. He seemed like a nice enough fella."

"He was. Milo—that's his assistant—is pretty broken up about it." Elizabeth looked up hopefully. "I don't suppose you have anything for grief?"

Amelanchier shrugged. "Just a handful of rocks."

"Rocks?"

"Yep. You take a handful of rocks and put them in a jar. Then once a week, you take one tiny pebble out of the jar and throw it away. When the jar is empty, why, you'll just about be over your grief."

Elizabeth digested the instructions. "I see," she said at last. "You mean that it just takes time."

"That's right. Time alone will do if you're short on rocks." She closed her eyes for a while, and her face relaxed from its usual smile into creases of age. "A-lord," she sighed. "I reckon I could use some bitters myself. How 'bout you?"

Elizabeth looked doubtful. Anything called "bitters" could not be very pleasant to drink, she thought. "What's in it?"

Amelanchier heaved herself off the bench and over to an old icebox beside the banister. She took two paper cups from a stack on top of it and poured dark brown liquid from a gallon milk jug into each. "Take a sip of that."

In the interests of science, thought Elizabeth. Taking a deep breath, she tasted it and was surprised to find that it was not bitter at all. "It's a little like root beer," she said wonderingly.

"That's the sassafras root bark," nodded Amelanchier. "You taste that, and the honey, which makes it sweet. There's other things in there, too, but I don't reckon your tongue told you that."

"Like what?" asked Elizabeth, holding her cup out for another helping.

"Comfrey and yarrow," said Amelanchier. "They're my favorites. And there's spikenard and Solomon seal and great blue lobelia, and about ten other things."

"It's really very good."

"Better for you than that old sody pop."

"What is it supposed to do?"

"Whatever you need done," Amelanchier declared. "Once you get the bad foods out of your system, the bitters will clean you out and keep you healthy."

Elizabeth was impressed. She wondered if the Appalachian studies department would consider a master's thesis on Amelanchier's brand of folk medicine. "How did you learn this?"

Amelanchier smiled. "Why, hit's Indian medicine. Old as the hills, but I don't reckon it'll do much for the poor in spirit, which is how I judge you to be right now."

Elizabeth sighed. "It's been awful," she admitted. "I've been trying not to worry about it, though."

"No, it's best to take things as they come," Amelanchier agreed. "Like they say in that old hymn: 'Farther along, we'll know all about it.'"

"I guess we will," said Elizabeth, taking the literal meaning. "The sheriff has been up here investigating. Or maybe not the sheriff himself, but some of his men. Of course, Victor claims to know it all now."

"Victor?"

"The one I told you about who is allergic to everything. He's full of himself today because he was out in the woods last night, and apparently he saw something. Of course he is keeping it to himself. By the

138

way, remember that ginseng cure you gave me for him? He wouldn't try it."

Amelanchier nodded. "Some folks won't. They're afraid you're trying to trick 'em. My gran'daddy used to say that believing nothing is just as foolish as believing everything."

"I wish I knew what to believe about Milo," sighed Elizabeth, still absorbed in her own troubles. "Ever since we got here, he has been so edgy, and now I can't talk to him at all. I know he's upset about Alex, but for heaven's sake, I didn't do it!"

Amelanchier reached under the bench and pulled out a paper bag. "If you're going to sit there a-twisting your hands like that, you might as well snap beans." She set the bag between them on the bench and handed Elizabeth a wooden bowl for her lap. "You know how, don't you?"

"Oh, sure," said Elizabeth, smiling at the memory of her Grandmother MacPherson, who wouldn't allow a frozen vegetable past her front door. "When we visited Granny's, this used to be my job." Deftly she stringed and separated a bean sheath, dropping the pieces into the bowl. Soon the snapping became a steady rhythm punctuating the flow of conversation.

"I guess it's awful of me to be worried about Milo and me when Alex has just died."

Amelanchier shook her head. "That's what they mean by life goes on. I reckon when you'uns get back to your college, he'll come around."

"Whenever that is," muttered Elizabeth.

"Why, your boss has got himself killed. Ain't you going home?"

"No. Milo is calling the university today to get permission to stay on."

"Well, then he'll be working hard, and that will be good for him. It'll wear out the grief. Hard work is the bitters of the spirit."

Elizabeth smiled. "I hope so."

After a moment's pause she added, "You haven't

been down to the dig site. Would you like to come and see what we're doing?"

"Naw, I don't care about seeing it," said Amelanchier. "I reckon I'm old enough to have known some of those folks, and I'll see them again in the hereafter. I can wait."

"It isn't so bad," mumbled Elizabeth apologetically. "I don't even think of the bones as human, somehow."

Amelanchier smiled bitterly. "Well, that ain't a problem they acquired lately. Folks around here didn't think of them as human even while they were alive." Her blue-veined hand shook a little as it dropped the bean shards into the bowl. She looked not at Elizabeth, but at the fold of green mountains framed by the porch railings and the clabbered sky. "Most of the county was Cullowhee land in the old days," she began slowly, as if remembering. "Flat land you could farm, down on the creek bottoms. But then the whites came in wanting land, and they reckoned to steal it."

The pile of beans fell from her lap. "If we had been regular old Indians, why, there wouldn't have been no trick to it atall. They would have marched us out to the desert, like they did the Cherokees—but we were different. Here we was a-talking English, living in regular old cabins, and praying to Jesus, just same as them. There was only one difference."

The old woman pressed her gnarled brown arm against Elizabeth's white one. "They called us people of color, and said we didn't have no rights. Got a law passed at the state capitol saying we couldn't vote nor hold office. Hell, we couldn't even testify in a court of law." She closed her eyes. "Then they started in with their lawyers and their judges, and they stole all the farmland away from our people— till all we got left is the ridges and the hollers. Now I reckon they want that, too!"

"Well, they won't get it!" said Elizabeth hotly.

"Er . . . that law *has* been repealed, hasn't it?" She twisted the snap bean between her wet fingers, feeling its wetness on her hands like blood.

"The law is gone, but the feelings stayed here right on." Amelanchier's eyes were dull pebbles, like uncut garnets in a creekbed.

Elizabeth shivered. Even in August it was not really warm on the mountain. The wind under the oaks bore the chill of autumn. Amelanchier sat still in her faded sundress, staring out at the mountains. After a while, she continued.

"No, the feelings ain't gone. When my young'uns were little, we'd go into town and I could buy them a sody pop at the grill, but they'd have to stand outside to drink it." She turned a level gaze on Elizabeth's reddened face. "Why do you think I'm a root doctor?"

Elizabeth swallowed the facile answers, woven around Amelanchier's Indian legend and a vague impression of her as a rustic version of a garden club lady. "Tell me."

"The Cullowhees always had a root doctor because no town doctor would see our people. It was passed down from my gran'daddy to me, because I was the seventh child of his seventh child. Some things we can't cure, and folks dies, but we did what we could, which is more than the white folks would."

"But surely . . ."

Amelanchier gave her a tight smile. "I didn't mean Dr. Putnam. He treats us like regular folks. But back before him, people died just because they . . . just because they . . ."

"I guess this is the other side of the Moonshine Massacre," Elizabeth put in quickly. "No wonder y'all resented the law up here."

The old woman waved her hand as if she were brushing away the thought. "That didn't have much to do with it. That moonshine business was them

141

spitting Harknesses, Bevel's kin. They're even worse than the blacksnake Harknesses."

From her folklore course, Elizabeth understood that mountain families with the same last name were often distinguished by a descriptive prefix. "Why blacksnake?" she asked.

Amelanchier snorted. "On account of Varner Harkness—he must be my age if he's a day. He used to chase girls through the briar patch waving a black snake over his head like a bullwhip."

Elizabeth wrinkled her nose. "What a charming family."

"I wouldn't give you one red cent for the whole lot of them."

"I know Bevel Harkness wants the strip miners to come in. Do the others agree with him?"

"I reckon they ought to, seeing as how their land is part of what the mining company wants. They'd get the money, and the rest of us would get the run-off down the creek."

"How can those people get away with it?" demanded Elizabeth. "Can't you turn them in for killing the sheriff's nephew?"

Amelanchier appeared not to have heard. "I think I'll pick ramps to go with my beans," she announced, hoisting an ark-shaped woven basket. Fashioned of blue and lavender reeds with a handle of twisted wood, the basket seemed as much a work of art as a utensil.

"How lovely!" breathed Elizabeth. "What's it made of?"

Amelanchier cradled the basket on her arm. "This here's grapevine, and that's wisteria, but—see this handle?" She pointed to the twisted branch. "That's the best part. It's kudzu."

"Kudzu? Ugh!" Elizabeth displayed the Southerner's dislike for that nuisance plant, imported to stop erosion, which strangled all the vegetation in its path. Kudzu even covered abandoned barns and houses with its jungle growth. People said that the only way to get rid of it was to burn it, roots and all.

"Yep. Kudzu is the ugliest, most trifling plant alive—but it makes a right nice basket handle, don't it?"

Elizabeth smiled. "And the Harknesses? Do they make right nice basket handles too?"

"I reckon they're good for something," said Amelanchier, pleased that Elizabeth had seen the parallel.

"I don't suppose anything could be done without the murder victim's body anyway," Elizabeth decided. "It was never found, was it?"

Amelanchier gripped the porch railing and crept down the steps. "You could lose something a lot bigger than a man in these hills," she said. "You ever pick ramps? It stinks like two days past judgment, but it sure does perk up beans. Come on."

Elizabeth watched the old woman stooping at the edge of the yard to uproot the wild onionlike plants. The smell from the broken stems was a mixture of garlic and onion, so strong that the tongue felt the heaviness of the odor. Amelanchier brushed the dirt from the white bulb roots and dropped them in the basket.

"Would you like me to do that?" asked Elizabeth, suddenly aware of how frail she looked.

Amelanchier smiled; her copper face shone with sweat. "Thank you, no. I like to keep my hand in. But I am taking it easier than what I used to." She nodded toward the cabin. "Comfrey rigged me up a generator powered by the creek water, so I don't have to fool with oil lamps. And I got a microwave that's real good to dry herbs in." Seeing Elizabeth's look of disbelief, she added, "I keep it hid when the tourists are about. They like to think I still live on poke salad and corn pone."

Elizabeth blinked. "But you do! I mean, what about the raccoon?"

"I love the old food when I'm up to fixing it, and I usually cook if Comfrey's coming by, but I'm like as not to have canned spaghetti and packaged cupcakes any other time." She shook her head. "It just don't do to let the tourists know. They like to think that time has passed us by up here on the ridge, just like the four-lane did. They need to believe the old ways are still around as much as they need the root medicine. So I keep my store food in the root cellar."

"But—tonight you're having beans and ramps?"

"Yep," said Amelanchier, winking. "And frozen pizza!"

Dear Bill,

I know you're going to find this out from the campus newspapers, but I thought I'd better give you more details than that. Alex Lerche has been murdered. I'm pretty sure he was killed by someone up here who wants the strip miners to get the Indians' land; probably the same person who trashed our computer. I don't want to go into all that right now. I just wanted you to know that I'm all right, that we're continuing the dig, and that I'm not coming home.

It isn't that I'm being ghoulish about wanting to stay and see who did it—which would be why *you* would stay—it's because of Milo. He is terribly upset over all this, and I honestly think that if we left, he'd finish the project by himself without even stopping to eat or sleep. He's being a perfect bear, too! I realize that men are supposed to contain their grief, but the fallout from all that suppression is very hard to live with. If you have any advice on how to cope with him without getting one's head bitten off, I wish you would let me know. He acts as if death has just been invented to torment him. He has cornered the market on suffering. I know I sound angry, but it is a frustrating feeling to care about someone and not be allowed to help them. Milo can't find "feelings" on his anatomy chart, so he won't admit that they exist!

I'm not giving up, though. By all means, write to me if you think you could be of any help, but don't come up here. I don't think Milo could take an amateur detective playing around with this case. We should be home in a week or so. You can be vague and reassuring with Mother and Dad for that long, can't you? Thanks!

Love,
Elizabeth

CHAPTER ELEVEN

PILOT BARNES seldom agreed with his brother-in-law about anything, be it fertilizer or Carolina basketball strategy. Watching Warren straddle a chair backwards and pontificate on every subject that came up set Pilot's teeth on edge. This murder case was no exception; Warren had a layman's compulsion to second-guess the police, as if his hours of viewing "Dragnet" and "Barnaby Jones" counted toward a degree in police science. He had heard about the case from Marcia, when Pilot was late coming home, and had called the next morning to pronounce the case a lucky break for Pilot career-wise. Having a big-time murder case to solve, without Duncan Johnson around to take credit for it, could be parlayed into a bid for the sheriff's job, according to Warren. Pilot didn't believe it. He saw it as an unlimited opportunity to screw up in Duncan Johnson's absence.

"Morning, Pilot," said Hamp McKenna, easing his way past the floorboard that creaked if you stepped on it. "I came to do a little paperwork, so if you need to go anywhere, I'll be here about an hour. I'd stay longer, but I've got a sick calf up home." He looked at Pilot appraisingly. "She looks better than you do, though."

Pilot squinted up at him with a sour smile. "I'll live."

"Lord, so will she, I hope! She's a purebred Charolais—cost me more than two car payments. You heard from Duncan yet?"

"No. He's still on the boat."

"Well, I hope he's catching more than we are. You solved the case yet?"

Pilot studied the geological survey map of the county, staring at it as if the lines would re-form to a profile of the murderer. He sighed. "I guess we just keep asking questions."

Hamp walked over to the map. "Pilot," he said slowly, "there's something you may not have thought of. Where did the murder take place?"

Pilot Barnes scowled at him. "You were right there with me when we went into the tent. You took the pictures yourself! Now what the hell do you mean asking me—"

Hamp shook his head impatiently. "No. I know what the death scene looked like. What I meant was: whose land is it on?"

Pilot's mouth hung open, frozen in midsyllable by this new possibility. "Why—church land." But he didn't sound sure about it.

"It's a good little ways from the church," Hamp reminded him.

"I didn't notice any fences around, either," Pilot grunted. "So you're saying—"

"Not for sure. But it is a possibility. The forest service land goes into that section of the county, but we don't know where the cutoff point is. Can you tell from the map?"

"Not for sure. But I don't have to be positive. Reasonable certainty ought to be enough!"

Hamp relaxed. "Yeah, I thought it would be. So, you gonna do it?"

Pilot set his jaw. "Absolutely. Screw Duncan Johnson. I'm calling in the FBI."

The phrase "calling in the FBI" had a magic ring to it that brightened their spirits at once. It summoned visions of television actors in business suits

147

driving up in dark green LTDs and solving the case in fifty-one minutes, with the trial thrown in as an afterthought before the closing credits. Pilot didn't suppose that it would be like that in real life, but nevertheless it was reassuring to know that a phone call to the number labeled "FBI" on Duncan Johnson's desk would bring to bear the power of the federal government in their backcountry murder case. This authority could be invoked because Hamp McKenna had thought of the one loophole that would involve them: reasonable certainty that the crime had occurred on federal land. Pilot dialed the number with a feeling of pleasant expectation.

It rang eight times.

Pilot pictured a suspect holding the entire FBI office at gunpoint. Lantern-jawed agents and their beautiful blond secretary staring courageously at the barrel of a .44 Magnum while the phone pealed away, unanswered. Pilot wondered who you called to rescue the FBI. Unable to think of an answer to that one, he kept sitting there letting the phone ring. Finally someone picked it up.

"Hello?" said a thin, piping voice.

Pilot took the receiver away from his ear and looked at it. "Is this the FBI?" he asked uncertainly.

"Yes, it is," the little voice assured him. "Just a minute." He heard the clunk of the phone being set down, and the voice yelling: "Daddy! Telephone!"

Pilot closed his eyes. To paraphrase his favorite beer commercial, it didn't get any worse than this. After several minutes' wait, the phone was picked up and a grown-up voice said: "Yello, FBI. This is Garrett."

Pilot hadn't planned out what he was going to say. In a halting voice he managed to explain about his murder case and the possibility of its having occurred on federal land. Agent Garrett listened to the deputy's entire explanation in an unhurried silence. Finally he said: "I'll come over and check it out. Give me directions."

In the background, Pilot could hear little voices demanding lemonade. He could stand it no longer. "Is this FBI headquarters?"

Agent Garrett laughed. "In a manner of speaking. The regional office is in Asheville, but since I'm assigned to this rural area, I just work out of my house. I go in twice a month to do the paperwork. Don't worry about the informality, Deputy. I get the job done."

Pilot hung up the phone. If it weren't for the unquestionably dead body on the slab, he could swear that Duncan Johnson had staged all this before he left.

Ron Garrett frowned speculatively as he peered at Pilot Barnes' map of the county. He ran his finger along a boundary line and then stopped, his finger poised above a smaller map he'd brought with him, but he couldn't seem to find the corresponding lines.

"What do you think?" asked the deputy anxiously. "Is that within federal land?"

Garrett shrugged. "It's close. I'd rather let my office have the final say-so on it, and even then there might have to be a survey. I guess we could check old courthouse records. But don't worry about it. You called me out to have a look, so the least I can do is view the site. You want to show me the way?"

"I can take you in the patrol car," Pilot offered.

"Nah. You ride with me. I have my kit in the trunk. Never know what we might need in the way of equipment." He turned to Hamp McKenna. "You're welcome to ride along too. Just watch where you sit in the back seat."

Hamp blinked. "Why? Evidence?"

"There's a model airplane back there. Belongs to my kid."

149

"So you're going to investigate this anyway?" asked Pilot.

"Sure. Why not? Maybe I can help you out with information on your suspects. You said they were from out of state, didn't you?"

"Most of them."

"No problem. We'll run their names through the computer and see what we get. Fingerprints, too, if you want."

Pilot nodded gratefully. He decided that Agent Garrett looked like a regular FBI person—tall, slender, well groomed, and dressed in sensible but fashionable outdoor clothes. He was sure that the car would also be an appropriately dark and expensive sedan. Once the deputy had recovered from the shock of the phone call, he had accepted this rural version of the FBI without too much trouble. Everything in the country was a little out of kilter as far as stereotypes went. The mailmen didn't dress in blue uniforms and drive white postal vans, the firemen drove their own cars to the fire, and FBI headquarters was a brick house with a carport. It just proved what Pilot had always known: he didn't live in the America you saw on television. He straightened his hat and followed the agent outside.

Milo entered the motel room like one entering a shrine. Alex's coffee cup still sat on the desk top beside the computer, and his scribbled notes littered the bed. It looked haphazard, but it wasn't. Alex would have known the location of every page of it. Mechanically Milo began to collect them into a pile. He supposed that they were his now, professionally speaking. Tessa would not want Alex's technical notes. Even now she must be parceling out his clothes and books, packing away the memory of Alex in little cardboard boxes for the Goodwill.

"You're dead, Alex," he said, as if there were someone there to be told.

It was Milo's first feeling of death as a personal loss; before, he had always reacted selfishly to the news of a death in his parents' circle of friends, affronted that his childhood world was changing irretrievably. When he was away at school, preoccupied with his own life, he subconsciously expected his hometown, his childhood acquaintances to stay the same. The death of his mother's cousin, the kind lady on the farm, had annoyed him not because he would miss her—he had not seen her since he was ten—but because it pushed his childhood farther into an unredeemable past. One by one his grade school teachers and parents' friends would die, until one day he would go home to find the small town urbanized beyond recognition and peopled by strangers. He remembered the feeling of isolation that that realization brought; it had come back. Alex had closed a door to Milo's college life, placing it firmly in the past tense, beyond recall. The present seemed narrower than ever.

What would he do now? Back at the university there would be a restrained meeting. Temporary measures would be taken to cover Alex's fall classes, and the dean would claim to be "taking the matter under advisement." Milo hoped it wouldn't mean starting over at another university. He banished the unworthy thought, wondering why even genuine grief must be tempered with selfishness. With a sigh, he sat down at the desk and flipped on the computer to finish Alex's project. That was a species of grief.

The screen was a luminous void. Milo opened the notebook to the columns of figures recorded in Elizabeth's spiky handwriting. She wanted Milo to confide in her. He could tell by the way she acted; but he wouldn't parade his grief to further a romance. What would she expect of him in the name of intimacy? Tears? A stirring resolution to track down the killer? Would Alex want that if it were someone he cared about? Would he want his death avenged?

Absently, Milo typed: "Should we catch the murderer?"

The words flashed on the screen in precise glowing letters. The machine hummed, and flashed its response: "Invalid command. Please try again or enter Help."

Agent Garrett frowned at the recently scrubbed camp table, still streaked with soaked-in blood. "A tomahawk, huh? I wonder what that means?"

"No fingerprints on a bark handle, for one thing," said Pilot Barnes.

Garrett nodded. "Okay. That might indicate pre-meditation. A tomahawk ... Didn't you say there were Indians around here?"

"There are Cullowhees," the deputy replied. "Some people don't think it's the same thing."

"Anyway they don't use tomahawks," Hamp pointed out. "They don't use much of nothing Indian."

"It wasn't an old one. It was one of the ones they sell at Cherokee, made in Taiwan, with plastic cords and dyed chicken feathers. But the rock was the real thing. It took a chunk out of the back of his head like grease going through a goose."

"Have you been able to trace ownership?" asked Garrett, ignoring the deputy's colorful bravado.

"Nope."

"I guess that isn't a job for a two-man force. There must be a couple of thousand tourists in and out of Cherokee every day, and every store on the strip sells them. My kids have one. But you might let me take it up to the lab anyway. They might be able to find something. But it's slim. I'd say your best bet would be to go for *cui bono.*"

"Motive, you mean," said Pilot, trying not to make it sound like a guess.

"Sure. Was there any particular reason for eliminating this individual?"

"When it comes to motive, we got too much of a good thing. The guy was working on a project to give this land to the Cullowhees, and keep some people from making a killing selling this land to a strip-mining company."

The FBI man smiled. "Maybe they made their killing anyway."

"Huh? Oh, I see. A real killing, you mean. Then, on a personal level, this fellow seems to have been having an affair with one of his assistants."

"Which one?"

"The girl. Her name is Mary Clare Gitlin. She was present at the time of the murder."

"Here, you mean?"

Pilot shrugged. "Claims she was out walking in the woods. The wife was here, too. And the deceased further gummed up the works by having a fight with one of the male students over some bones in a museum."

"Don't forget the Cullowhees," Hamp reminded him.

"The Indians? I thought he was helping them. Why should they kill him?"

"Because they're Cullowhees," said Pilot with a tight smile. "You're not from around here, are you?"

Garrett sighed. "Everybody says that. And no, I'm not. It's FBI policy not to assign anyone to his own hometown."

"Too bad. Sometimes it helps to know the background things," said Pilot. "Take the Cullowhees, for instance. Those folks are so mean they must've been weaned on snake venom. Ain't a man in the valley that hasn't seen the inside of our jail two or three times. Summer's the worst. They get so likkered up they'd stab their own mothers."

"Tell him about the parade that time," Hamp prompted.

"That was a few years back, but I don't reckon folks'll ever forget it. Bunch of Cullowhees got piss-eyed drunk at a poker game up here and killed some joker they claimed was cheating. He was a white man, too. Lord knows how he got in the game in the first place."

"Likely they figured to take *his* money," said Hamp.

"Yeah. Well, they stabbed him in the belly, and went on with the game while he bled to death. And then they strung him up in chains behind a pickup truck and drug him down the highway to Laurel Cove."

"Right down Main Street," said Hamp. "And there was about ten of them a-sitting in the back of that pickup, waving like it was the Easter parade."

"I heard it was four," frowned Pilot.

"Well, whatever," said Garrett quickly. "I guess those people aren't around any more after that."

Hamp laughed. "You'd be wrong, then. They got the driver of the truck by his license number, but he claimed not to remember who the others were. Never did charge anybody with the murder."

The agent shook his head. "Okay," he said at last. "Who do you think did it?"

Pilot hesitated. "Well . . . seeing as how it happened in Sarvice Valley, I'd have said the Cullowhees right off, but it's a little too neat to be them."

Hamp nodded. "You expect them to take somebody out in a brawl, not sneak up behind 'em like that. And they'd probably mess him up more, too."

"Who did you say these people are?"

They shrugged. "Nobody knows," said Pilot. "People say they're part Portuguese or African or Inca. I've heard they're descendants of the Lost Colony."

"Nobody knows who *they're* related to," said Hamp. "But the devil himself is related to *them.*"

Milo slid the replacement disk into the computer

and prepared to add the Cullowhee data to the existing file of Indian data. Since there were only twenty-five skulls in the present sample, he decided to record each separate measurement as well as the final number. It might be useful for comparison later. Elizabeth had made it easy for him by labeling each set of measurements and putting them in groups according to which tool was used to take the measure.

He would enter all his figures, calculate a standard deviation and a range of variation in millimeters. When all the data were entered on the disk, he would call up the university computer to compare his data with the existing discriminate function charts. About an hour's work, Milo decided. Maybe more if he were especially careful with his numbers and decimal points. He might as well take his time, since the skulls were in the sheriff's office labeled as evidence. He hoped they'd be back by the next day. If not, he and Elizabeth would begin to measure other bones that might be helpful in the identification process: humerus bones and femurs. If they suspected that one of the bodies belonged to the sheriff's nephew or some other non-Cullowhee, they could have fluorine tests run on it. No point in thinking about that until he got the skulls back.

Milo sprawled back in his chair, punching in numbers with his two index fingers. Since the process required a minimum of thought, he allowed his mind to sort the events of the past few days, looking for some detail he might have missed before. What about Victor? Milo had written him off as a pudgy fool impersonating an intellectual, but he had been genuinely angry about that scene with Alex. Of course he minded being humiliated; he told lies to make himself seem more important. But surely people do not kill for so slight an insult. Yes, they do, he thought, but he hoped that had not been the case. To lose Alex over something so trivial would be heartbreaking.

After nearly two hours of steady work, Milo finished updating the Indian file. Remembering the break-in, he inserted a blank disk and made a backup copy to take back to the site. No one would threaten the project again if he could help it. When the copy had been safely tucked away, Milo checked the time and decided that he could still compare his lists to the university's data. They weren't expecting him at the site until dinner time; maybe not even then. He hadn't eaten much in the past few days.

Milo set the telephone headset into the plastic cradle and called up the campus system. "Request," said the screen in glowing green letters.

"Archaeological File #307-Lerche," Milo typed.

"Enter user I.D."

Milo tapped out, "D-i-g-g-e-r." The word appeared before him correctly spelled.

The machine paused as if digesting this tidbit. A moment later, it replied: "Enter password."

"Carter," Milo said aloud, suiting his action to the word. They had arranged the password between them. "Digger" symbolizing archaeology, and then "Carter" in honor of the man who discovered the tomb of Tutankhamen. The password would not appear on the screen; that was a standard safety precaution.

For a moment the screen stayed blank, presumably while the university computer contemplated Howard Carter. Then it spat out: "Access denied. Password invalid."

"I hit the wrong damn key," muttered Milo, typing in "Carter" with painstaking slowness.

This time the computer was positive. It shot back: "Access denied. Password invalid."

Milo began to wonder if the old King Tut curse was still in effect. Why the hell was he getting the runaround? He typed in "Howard Carter," just to be thorough. The machine wasn't having any. "Access denied. Password invalid."

Milo snatched the telephone receiver from its cradle and called the university. All university prefix numbers were the same, and he had called the computer terminal often enough to remember the four-digit extension number. He supposed that the system was down, but he was going to yell at somebody about it.

"Computer center," said a bored voice in a noisy room.

"Yeah. This is Milo Gordon, Dr. Lerche's assistant. Let me speak to Jamie."

"Jamie went home early today, man. He was up till all hours last night fixing the bugs in a program. Can I help?"

"Is the computer down?"

"Nope. It's doing fine. How about yourself?"

"I need to call up some data from the mainframe, and your damned jukebox keeps telling me access denied."

"That's funny," mused the voice. "Does it say why?"

"Says invalid password, but I used the same one we always had."

There was a brief pause. "Hold on a second." Milo heard the phone being put down. Idly, he wondered whether some hacker in the C.S. department had rigged the computer to refuse *all* passwords. Could somebody do that?

"Hello, Milo. Are you sure you're using the right password?"

"Of course," snapped Milo. "I've used it a hundred times. And I tried more than once today, so don't try to tell me I made a typing error."

"No, I wasn't thinking of that. Tell me, when was the last time that you used that password?"

"Well, I haven't tried to call up the university system since before Alex went back to—" An awful possibility suddenly occurred to him. "Has Alex been in lately?"

"Yeah. Earlier in the week. He was talking to Jamie about some trouble you guys had up there with vandalism. I was sorry to hear it. You got it fixed?"

"Uh-huh. Listen, did Alex change the password?"

"I don't know. He might have. Can't you ask him?"

Milo didn't want to go into it with this guy on the phone whose name he couldn't remember. "No. I'm here alone. Can you give me the new password?" He should have realized that Alex would have changed the password. It was the most logical thing he could have done after the break-in.

"Gee, I'm sorry, Milo. I don't have access to it." The voice was pleasantly neutral, unaware of the news about Alex. "But if you'll call back tomorrow, Jamie can get it for you."

"Yeah, sure. Maybe I'll try a few guesses meanwhile."

"Well, good luck."

Milo hung up, resisting the urge to slam the telephone into its cradle. Another stumbling block. What would Alex choose for a password? He called the system again.

"Request."

"Archaeological File #307-Lerche."

"Enter user I.D."

"Digger."

"Enter password."

It wasn't Howard Carter. Maybe another archaeologist. "Schliemann," Milo typed.

"Access denied. Password invalid."

He repeated the process with Sir Arthur Evans, several variations of Teilhard de Chardin, and finally, in utter desperation, Indiana Jones, but the computer would have none of it. Access was politely, but firmly, denied.

Milo gave up. He could settle this tomorrow. At

worst, this was a minor inconvenience to which he was overreacting, but his anger wouldn't settle. He typed: "You are not going to stop me from finishing this project, damn it!" and flipped off the machine before it could register another coldly mindless reply.

CHAPTER TWELVE

IT WAS GOING to be another hot day. The sky was blazing blue by eight o'clock, not a breath of air stirring. The parched clay in the clearing was dead land, like a scar surrounded by the living forest. Elizabeth and Jake sat on a fallen log at the edge of the clearing, less than enthusiastic about the day's work ahead.

"This place is going to be an oven," said Elizabeth, tossing a pebble past her sneakered foot. "Can't we pack it in?"

"Hey," Jake protested. "This is my first day as site manager and already half my crew is mutinying."

"Make it unanimous," said Victor, flopping down beside him. "I just filled up the water jug, but don't expect it to last past nine o'clock."

"It'll probably evaporate from the heat," said Elizabeth. "What if we pass out from sunstroke?"

"Oh, come on! We're in the mountains! I'll bet it isn't even ninety. You're feeling the humidity, that's all. Anyway, we said we were going to finish this project, remember?"

"But the sheriff's department took my skulls!" said Elizabeth. "What am I supposed to do?"

"I'll assign you to something else. Don't worry, there's plenty of work to be done—especially if the day people don't show up."

Victor took a swig from the water jug. "Mary Clare's gone, Milo's back in a nice air-conditioned motel room, and we're stuck out here—"

"Like birds in the wilderness," Elizabeth nodded.

"Look," said Jake in tones of strained patience. "If

you want to go back to the church, fine. But I'm going to stay up here and work, particularly since I think this site ought to be guarded. Now, if you want to risk being down there alone, go ahead."

"I'll stay," said Elizabeth in a small voice.

"I suppose somebody has to keep an eye on things here," said Victor grudgingly. "But if I get sun poisoning . . ."

"We'll just add you to the sample," smiled Jake. "You did say you were part Indian, didn't you?"

They worked in silence for most of the next hour, troweling, measuring, and marking various points about the site. Elizabeth stopped periodically to apply more baby oil to her arms and face, saying that she had no desire to look like a radish in the interests of science. A little after nine, when the sun had sharpened the angle of its rays on the clearing, they heard voices in the woods. Elizabeth looked questioningly at Jake, but he motioned for her to keep working. A moment later he heard the rustle of underbrush near the tent, and Comfrey Stecoah emerged, holding a hunting rifle.

"Y'all just go on with what you were doing," he said softly, fading back into the bush.

Elizabeth went on tying string to a wooden stake in what seemed to her like slow motion, as the indistinguishable babble of voices grew louder. Suddenly the words became distinct, and she recognized one of the speakers. "Jake!" she called out loudly for Comfrey's benefit. "It's the day workers! And we're *very glad* to see them, aren't we?"

"Yes!" Jake called back. "They-are-our-friends." He glanced over his shoulder to see if the message had been received.

Five diggers from the local archaeological group came straggling in from the trail. Jake and Elizabeth greeted them effusively, casting anxious glances back toward the underbrush. Victor unscrewed the water jug and peered into it, frowning.

As soon as the workers had been settled into their usual tasks, Jake excused himself and headed for the bush. "What are you doing here?" he hissed.

Comfrey Stecoah emerged from behind a tree to the right of him. "I'm over here," he said.

"Yeah—with a gun. Why?"

"Why, I'm just looking out for you, Little Beaver," said Comfrey with an easy smile.

Jake scowled. "Look, Mr. Stecoah, I think that gun could cause more problems than it solves. I think we're safe up here in broad daylight."

"Do you, now?" Comfrey rubbed his finger speculatively along the line of his jaw. "Seems to me like I snuck up on y'all with a loaded rifle. If my intentions had been evil, I reckon I could'a blowed you all to kingdom come, with nobody being the wiser."

Jake had to admit he had a point. The killer was still loose in the woods, presumably. What could it hurt to have some volunteer protection? The sheriff's department certainly hadn't offered any. "Okay," he said. "I guess it would be okay for you to stick around." He eyed the rifle nervously. "Just don't wave that thing around. You'll make us feel like a chain gang."

Comfrey nodded. "I don't want to scare you folks, but somebody has to protect my people's stake in this land. Somebody wants us to lose this land, and he won't stop at killing just one of you. Not for the money this land is worth."

"Well . . . why don't you come out there and sit down?"

"I don't want to be a target, boy," Comfrey said in a pitying voice. "I'm your guard." He looked serious. "I wanted to tell you'uns how sorry I am that the doctor got killed. He was a good man, and he was trying to help us."

"Yeah," said Jake softly. "He was okay."

"I don't reckon he'd want any harm to come to the

162

rest of you'uns, so you go on back out there, and I'll see that it don't."

Jake blinked. "Okay. Just be careful with that thing!"

Comfrey smiled. "I ain't never killed anything by accident."

Victor troweled away, careful not to expose his upturned buttocks to the "loaded bush." He was sweating profusely. How long had it been since his last trip to the water jug? Last time he had drawn some meaningful looks from the trenches, and he was sure that if he approached the water jug again, something caustic would be said. Naturally, no one understood his delicate metabolism, or the nature of his sensitive skin. He oughtn't to be out in the hot sun at all really, he told himself. Victor had long been convinced that discomfort was a bona fide illness. Unfortunately, most people did not subscribe to this theory, so for their benefit, he usually attributed his indisposition to something more acceptable, such as a migraine. It was nearly hot enough to warrant one, but Victor was determined to stick it out. He saw himself as second-in-command at the site now, and the increased feeling of self-importance compensated for the discomfort of the work. Perhaps after the next development (he allowed himself to fantasize Jake's arrest and departure in leg-irons) he might become site manager himself.

Victor began to plan a letter to his parents informing them of his new, exalted position. He considered himself the intellectual hope of his hopelessly bourgeois family. His mother's emotional life centered around the characters on the one-o'clock soap opera, and his father's imagination was limited to believing that the Reds would someday win the world series. Victor considered it his duty to shock them with bizarre opinions whether he believed them or not. By the time he had finished seventh grade, his parents had decided that he was a genius. They were now waiting, a little nervously, to see what he would make of himself. The archaeological dig was a perfect example of something Victor *would* do for a summer, instead of going home and getting a job to earn tuition money. He had announced his plans by saying that he would spend the summer robbing graves. Victor smiled, thinking of his parents' reaction to the news of his promotion: he doubted if they would know what he was talking about.

"We're out of water!" called one of the day crew.

"Well, go and get some," someone shot back.

"Hey, I didn't even get any yet!" the digger protested, upturning the empty jug. "I'd probably drop in my tracks."

"I'll go," Victor heard himself saying. His reverie about becoming site manager had put him in a good mood, and besides, if he went back to the church he could drink all the water he wanted before refilling the jug. The walk in the woods would be cooler, too, than grubbing in the hot sun in the clearing. "You go on back to what you were doing, and I'll bring the water. No trouble." He managed to sound as if he were making a gallant sacrifice for the welfare of his troops.

The troops sneered. "You used most of it anyway!"

He ambled out of the clearing to catcalls and demands that he hurry back.

The woods were somewhat cooler, but that was the limit of Victor's aesthetic appreciation of nature. Everything green looked like poison ivy, and everything flowering was an allergy suspect. To Victor, a simple woodland walk took on the proportions of a minefield crossing. Victor patted his pockets. Maybe he should take an antihistamine when he got back to the church. Where were they? He must have left them back in his toilet articles kit with his green pills, sunscreen, asthma medicine, and the other antidotes to the immediate world. He sneezed, and glared suspiciously at a small yellow flower blooming beside the path. He advanced toward it, intending to grind it into the dirt, but then he remembered the pollen that would be sent into the air from shaking it and turned aside.

Someone was watching him.

"Hello," stammered Victor to the vaguely human outline concealed in shrubbery. "Are you walking toward the church? I'm going back to get water." He held up the water jug. "It's empty. Oh, you have one too," he said upon seeing his companion more clearly. "Oh? It isn't water? What's in there? Nothing alcoholic, I trust. Oh. Cider. I've heard that cider is good for allergies. Oh, no, really I couldn't. It's very kind of you to offer, but . . . well, if you're sure. Perhaps just a taste. It's an oven out there in the clearing."

He took the stoneware jug, hooking his thumb through the circular handle, and held it up to drink from, in what he imagined to be mountaineer fashion. The uncorked jug sent a great wave of cider down Victor's throat, so that he felt something feathery hit his throat, but not in time to spit it out. He was just opening his mouth to ask what it was when he felt his throat being stabbed from within, and cold ripples of numbness began to encircle the ache.

"It's a bee," he rasped. "I'm allergic." He opened his eyes and found himself alone on the path. The trees around him began a slow horizontal rotation, as if they, too, were walking away.

Victor's heart thudded against his ribs. His sweat was cold. ". . . Have to take a shot," he mumbled to himself. "Bee kit . . ." Was this the way to the church? He couldn't tell because the path was spinning. Nothing was clear except the pinging little pain in his throat. He listened to the pain for a while.

A new sensation, seeming to come from far away,

penetrated his consciousness. He could not swallow. Victor gasped for breath, tugging at the neck of his T-shirt. Dimly he realized that the bee sting in his throat was causing the tissue to swell and closing the air passage to his lungs. It felt a bit like an asthma attack. You strained and strained but nothing reached your lungs. Victor tried to think of a way to breathe without using his throat. He was still puzzling over this riddle in physiology when the spinning path became a blur, and he fell facedown into the weeds, clutching at them to keep from being swept away. He shut his eyes until the darkness filled his brain, and then he was still.

"Where is Victor?" asked Elizabeth, looking around. "He's certainly taking his time with that water."

"He'll come strolling in about lunchtime with some story about a headache," grumbled Jake. "I should have known better than to let him go for water."

"I wonder what possessed him to study archaeology?"

"It sounds a lot more romantic than it is," said Jake. "He probably has visions of strolling through a well-landscaped jungle and coming upon an abandoned Mayan temple just waiting to be discovered."

One of the day crew shook his head. "Nah. He figures that when he's the head man, he'll get somebody else to do the spade work."

The work continued for another hour, as the sun rose higher in the sky. It cleared the tops of the surrounding trees and blazed at them with white heat. Elizabeth dabbed at her forehead with a tissue. "Gosh, it's hot out here," she remarked to Jake. "I'm getting nearly as brown as you are."

Jake had taken off his shirt and was troweling in the trench next to her. He had wrapped his red bandanna around his head for a sweatband, but a few trickles slipped past it and slid down the sides of his face. He held his arm up against Elizabeth's to compare tans. "I've got a considerable head start, Blue-Eyes," he grinned.

Elizabeth giggled. "With that thing around your head, you look like an Apache."

He grunted. "You mean I look like Jeff Chandler, I suppose?"

"What?"

"Jeff Chandler played Cochise in the movie *Broken Arrow*. When most people say Apache, that's what they mean."

Elizabeth thought about it. "Was Jimmy Stewart in it?"

"Yep. He was the Indian agent."

"I guess you're right then. It's too hot to think. Where *is* Victor?"

"Where's the water? you mean."

She sighed. "Well, he is a pig to leave us without any. Especially since he drank most of it to begin with."

"That's Victor. What are our problems compared to millions of his?"

Elizabeth threw down her trowel. "I give up! I'll go after the water myself!"

"Victor took the jug," one of the diggers pointed out.

"Well, I'll find him and bring it back. Or I'll get a milk jug from the church. I am going to get some water up here. And when I find Victor, I'm going to tell him exactly what I think of him." She scrambled up the clay bank and dusted off the legs of her jeans.

"Elizabeth! Wait!" Jake looked worried. "Remember what we said about not getting separated."

"Oh, stop it! Victor is goofing off. I won't give him the satisfaction of getting worried about him! If I'm not back in twenty minutes, you can send the cavalry after me."

"Wait! Wait!" he called as she stalked off. "Don't you want to take . . . er . . ." He pointed to the shrubbery. "*Him* with you?"

Elizabeth gave him a look of complete exasperation. "Twenty minutes, okay?" And she was gone.

Elizabeth was careful where she walked, trying to make as little noise as possible. She was not trying to sneak past some monster lurking in the woods; her thoughts were on the deer they had glimpsed that morning on the way to the site. "There are lots of animals in the woods," Jake told her, "but unless you're quiet, you won't see them." She had followed his instructions and watched the underbrush carefully, delighted when a log turned out to be a fat groundhog having his breakfast. Now she tried to concentrate on sighting a rabbit or a fawn in order to keep her mind off lower forms of life, such as insects, snakes, and Victor.

He really was impossible, she thought. He had no more sense of responsibility than a groundhog. Was that a groundhog? She bent down to inspect a clump of bushes; no, it really was a log this time. She heard a skittering a few feet from the path and decided that it was a rabbit running for cover. At least the plants didn't hide. She spent the next hundred yards trying to identify the plants along the path, and mentally rehearsing the tongue-lashing she was going to give Victor.

". . . Selfish, infantile, neurotic . . ." Elizabeth stopped short.

In the weeds ahead she saw a patch of bright blue. Victor's trousers? What a funny place to sleep, Elizabeth thought, as the truth registered farther back in her mind. "Oh, no," she whispered.

Victor lay facedown in the weeds, still clutching at a stalk of broom sedge. His legs were spread at a convulsive angle, but he was quite still. Elizabeth was glad that she could not see his face.

"Victor," she said softly, edging closer to the body. She wondered what had happened; there didn't seem to be any blood. A stroke? Tentatively, she stretched out her hand. He might still be alive. His cheek felt cool, though. Elizabeth knelt and peered into Victor's swollen face, and then she was sure.

To Elizabeth, shocked into slow motion by the sight of the body, it seemed that she stood for hours in the clearing contemplating the stubble on Victor's chin, the water jug resting in a clump of knotweed, and the sound of birds far above her. Actually, only a few minutes passed before fear snapped her out of her reverie and sent her running back toward the site.

Jake looked up as she came crashing through a patch of thistles. "Will you be quiet? Do you want Mr. Stecoah to mistake you for a buffalo?" He saw her face and his smile faded. "What's wrong?"

"Victor's dead," gasped Elizabeth, sinking down on the log.

"How? Same as Alex?"

She shook her head. "I couldn't tell. There's no sign of a wound."

Jake turned away. "Okay. That's it," he muttered. He turned to the diggers staring up at him from the trenches. "Listen up!" he said, unnecessarily, for he had their full attention. "There has been an accident, and I'm stopping the dig. Everybody go back to the church, but don't leave. The police may need to talk to you."

"Stopping the dig?" someone said. "What's Milo going to say?"

"I don't much care," said Jake. "As long as there is someone left for him to say it to."

Elizabeth looked around. "Where is Comfrey Stecoah?"

"I haven't seen him since before you left. Let's find out."

They searched down the hill, away from the path, in the direction they had last seen Comfrey Stecoah. "We'd better yell for him," said Elizabeth. "I want to make sure he knows it's us."

After a few intervals of hoarse shouting, Comfrey Stecoah appeared, carrying his rifle in the crook of his arm and fastening his belt.

"Where were you?" Jake demanded.

"Call of nature. Didn't want to go so close to the burying ground. What are you'uns making such a racket about?"

"Something has happened to one of our diggers," said Elizabeth.

"That fat boy that went for water?" They nodded. "Ambush?"

"I don't think so," said Elizabeth. "I didn't see any blood or anything. He's just ... dead."

"We're all going back to the church now," said Jake firmly. "Would you come with us, please?"

"Have you reported it?"

They both looked at Elizabeth. "Not yet," she said. "I came back as soon as I found him. Shouldn't someone stay with the body?"

"I will," said Jake.

"Not by yourself, you won't!" said Elizabeth indignantly. "Look, why don't I go back with the day crew, and you and Mr. Stecoah guard the body. There are so many of us that I'm sure we'll be safe. I can get Randall to drive me to a phone so that I can report this."

Jake hesitated.

"You don't know that it was murder," Elizabeth reminded him. "Victor wasn't all that healthy."

"Okay, okay. Get out of here before I come to my senses. We'll stay with the body. Go on."

Elizabeth looked back. "Jake, should I call Milo?"

"Ask Mr. Barnes to stop by and tell him. I don't

want us split up for any longer than we have to be. I think you'll be safe in the church with the diggers. Anyway, we can all walk back together as far as . . ."

As far as the body, Elizabeth thought. "I wish there were another way back."

They filed past the body in silence, most of the diggers averting their eyes, respecting the privacy of the dead. Elizabeth looked again at Victor and tried to think of something kind, something that she would miss. When this proved futile, she fell back upon the hope that he had not suffered.

When they were out of sight of the death scene, they began to talk in low voices about what they would do when they got back to the church, and about Milo's plans for the excavation. Finally the speculation trailed off into a despondent silence. As they emerged from the woods into the churchyard, one of the diggers gasped and pointed to a man walking toward them.

"It's all right," said Elizabeth after a moment's scrutiny. "He's a deputy."

What a solemn bunch these archaeologists are, thought Daniel Hunter Coltsfoot as he studied their grim faces. Mentally he prescribed an herb tonic for the lot of them. "Hi!" he said with professional friendliness. "I was hoping I'd catch you on lunch break."

"Who called you?" asked Elizabeth, looking around for the squad car.

"Nobody," said Dummyweed. "I just dropped in on the off chance of catching you here, and—" The implication of her question struck him. "Why?" he asked hoarsely.

"There's been another death."

The erstwhile deputy took a step back. "Now look, I just came up to invite you guys to our craft fair. I'm not . . . I mean—"

Elizabeth wasn't listening. "Randall will show you where the body is while the rest of us go to a phone to report it. I'll tell Mr. Barnes you're here."

"But I don't like bodies!" Dummyweed was protesting as Randall led him away.

"All right, which car are we taking?" asked Elizabeth briskly. "I think three of us should stay here in the church. One of you can go with me to telephone. Where's Robin?"

"She went inside the church—oh, there she is."

A slender girl in olive khaki slacks appeared on the porch. "I found this on the table," she told Elizabeth, handing her a piece of notebook paper.

Elizabeth unfolded the note and read it aloud: "Sorry I missed you. I came back for my guitar. I'd stay to lunch, but I want to get back to MacDowell because Special Collections closes at five. And anyway, I've tasted y'all's cooking. Best, Mary Clare." Elizabeth lowered the note. "So she was here today too."

"Are you going to tell the sheriff?" asked Robin.

Elizabeth nodded. "If Victor wasn't murdered, it won't matter. And if he was—I'd better!"

CHAPTER THIRTEEN

THE MOTEL ROOM was just as he had left it. Since the vandalism episode, Milo had always unlocked the door holding his breath, expecting a scene of wreckage within. He felt guilty that he had not stayed to guard the room as Alex had suggested, but subsequent events had eclipsed the destruction of the computer. Milo felt that he was needed more at the site. As soon as he got this password business straightened out, he intended to go back and supervise the digging. He glanced at his watch. Jamie should be in by now, he decided, picking up the phone.

After a few moments, Jamie's voice came on the line, as calm and unhurried as always. "Milo! The news about Alex came out in the paper today. I'm really sorry to hear about it."

"Yeah," said Milo awkwardly. He never knew whether to accept the sympathy as consolation or to agree about what a shame it was. "I'm finishing the project, Jamie. At least, I'm trying to."

"That's right. He changed the password, didn't he? He told me about the trouble you had up there."

"It's okay now," said Milo, in no mood to chat. "What's the new password?"

Jamie hesitated. "Milo, we're not supposed to give those things out over the phone."

"Jamie, it's all right. It's *me*. You want to ask me a trick question? You want me to describe your office?"

"I know it's you, Milo," said Jamie patiently. "But the phone might be tapped."

"Look, if anybody wanted the password, they could probably break into the computer and get it! Anybody except me, that is! It's all I can do to make those things work *with* the password. Now, I know he used some archaeologist's name, because he always did. Which one?"

Jamie sighed. "Hold on."

Milo waited, tapping his fingers on the table and wondering who Jamie's boss was, in case he had to go up the whole damn bureaucracy to get the password. In a few minutes, Jamie was back on the line. "I can't say the password on an open phone line," he said, "but I can give you a hint."

Milo closed his eyes. "A hint," he groaned. "What is it?"

"I think he once had a dog named this."

Milo remembered an old black Labrador retriever; his picture was still on the pine table in Alex's den. Alex told stories about trying to housebreak the pup in a student apartment when he was an undergrad, and so he had named him ... Leakey! Milo smiled at the pun: the incontinent puppy named after the great paleoanthropologist Louis B. Leakey. "I got it, Jamie," he said quickly. "Thanks!"

He tapped through the well-worn formula, entered the password twice, and was relieved to see the title page of the file appear on the screen. He bypassed the introductory text and called up the chart itself, the thousand measurements of Plains Indian bones that Alex had spent his life classifying. The twenty-five Cullowhee skulls were little more than a footnote to the bulk of Alex's research, but in statistical data, every little bit helped. Milo typed in the command to compare the two groups of skulls. Line by line they appeared in glowing green letters. Milo stared at them as if the computer had spelled out Balshazzar's doom on the wall in Babylon. The numbers were entirely different.

Entirely different.

The Cullowhee numbers were not within the range established for American Indians. Milo dived for the notebook and checked the computer's figures against the numbers written down by Elizabeth. Perhaps he had miscopied them. *All of them?* his mind sneered back. He ran his finger down the page, checking number against number. They were all correct. Correctly incorrect, he amended. All the numbers were completely out of range. Elizabeth had done the measurements wrong. Every single one of them.

Milo flipped off the computer, resisting the urge to put his fist through the screen. She's only a beginner, he told himself. You can't expect her to be perfect. She had asked him again and again to check her work. And I was too busy, thought Milo disgustedly. Well, at least that explained what Alex had wanted to see him about the night he died. Alex had checked the skulls, and had found out that Elizabeth didn't know what she was doing. Obviously, he had wanted Milo to give her another lesson.

It wouldn't cost them too much time, Milo told himself. Then he remembered that the skulls had been impounded by the sheriff's department. Until the measurements were done correctly, the project was at a standstill. Milo swore. He would have to go and get the skulls back.

It was a short walk from the motel to the sheriff's office. Everything in Laurel Cove was a short walk, Milo told himself without amusement. He had spent the time wondering whether it would be necessary to hire a lawyer to get the skulls back, and if he ought to check with Bill about it. Lawyers would take more time than he had, he decided, wondering if Pilot Barnes would respond better to bullying or pleading. He was trying to decide which one he could best manage when he pushed open the door to the sheriff's office. The fact that Pilot Barnes seemed to be expecting him put him off stride before he could do either.

"Reckon they called you, too," the deputy remarked.

"Who?" said Milo.

"Your folks at the church. I'm going out there now. You want to follow me?"

Milo froze. "What happened?"

"You don't know? Well, what did you come in here for?"

"Never mind," said Milo, not believing he'd said it. "What's wrong?"

"There's been a death up there. Might be natural causes though."

Milo said carefully, "Was it a woman?"

"Young man. Name of Victor Bassington. You want to go out there? I'm leaving as soon as the coroner gets here."

Milo was ashamed of the feeling of relief he had felt upon hearing Victor's name. "Of course I'll come. Let me get the car."

The Sarvice Valley Road was beautiful on a summer day, but Pilot Barnes was in no mood to appreciate postcard scenes. Those damned tourists had become a personal crime wave in the space of two weeks. The fact that Dr. Putnam was enjoying it all did not improve his disposition in the slightest.

"What do you reckon it'll be this time, Pilot?" The coroner cackled. "Scalping?"

Pilot refused to be drawn. "Heart attack most likely," he growled.

"You're no fun," Dr. Putnam pouted. "Heard from Duncan yet?"

"Yeah. He's on his way back. But they're stopping at his sister's in Winston-Salem first. He says that if the FBI is working on the case, there's no point in ruining his vacation over it."

"Watch the curve here," murmured the doctor, sensing that Pilot Barnes' frustration had localized in his right foot. "Slow down. Have you called that FBI fellow yet about this new development?"

"Nope. Don't know that it is one. That's for you to find out."

"That young fellow behind us seems pretty upset about it."

"Yeah, but he doesn't think it's the Cullowhees. And he was a lot more upset until he found out who it was."

"How's his alibi?"

Pilot Barnes gave him a pained look. "Dr. Putnam," he sighed. "Couldn't you at least pronounce the fellow dead before you go hunting up suspects?"

Milo caught up with them as they reached the steps of the church. "Why are you going in there?" he asked.

"To find out where the body is," said the deputy. "And to talk to the girl who found him."

"Can I come with you?" asked Milo.

Pilot shrugged. "Long as you don't get in the way."

Everyone looked up as they entered the church. Elizabeth, who had been writing something, put the paper away. "I'm the one who found the body," she told the deputy. "It's on the path between here and the site. Would you like me to show you?"

"Where is Jake?" Milo interrrupted, forgetting his promise to be unobtrusive.

"He's out there," said Elizabeth. "He and Comfrey Stecoah were going to stay with the body. Oh, and your deputy is with them," she added to Pilot.

Pilot stared. He knew that McKenna was off today. Suddenly he realized which deputy she meant. "What's Dum—Coltsfoot doing here?" he demanded.

Elizabeth shrugged. "Something about a craft fair. Anyway, he's up there too. Would you like me to take you?"

Pilot shook his head. "Sounds like there's enough of a crowd already," he grunted, turning to leave.

Milo started to go with him.

"Is it true that we're calling off the dig?" asked one of the day crew.

Milo stiffened. "Where'd you hear that?" he asked more calmly than he felt.

"Jake," murmured Elizabeth apologetically.

Milo glared at her. "I'll talk to him later. And to you." He walked out, slamming the door.

Elizabeth managed to say, "This isn't my day," before she burst into tears.

In the presence of a body, Dr. Putnam lost all his facetiousness and became a skilled professional. He knelt beside Victor's body, measuring and probing, oblivious to the conversations going on around him.

"Am I going to get paid for this?" Dummyweed hissed at Pilot Barnes. "This is the second time I've had to babysit a corpse, and I'm not even on the payroll!"

"I thought you were supposed to look out for us!" Jake growled at Comfrey Stecoah.

"And I thought I told you to stay together!" said Milo. "What's this about you calling off the dig, anyway?"

Comfrey Stecoah scowled. "Scared you off, have they?"

"You stay out of this!" snapped Milo.

Dr. Putnam looked up. "Could y'all please quit!" he asked mildly.

They looked down at the corpse, remembering the presence of death. "Sorry," muttered Milo. "Can you tell anything yet?"

"Insofar as I can hear myself think, yes," drawled the coroner. "I'll have to get the state lab to back me up on this, but I'm sure enough to make a guess."

"Is it natural causes?" asked the deputy anxiously.

"Well, he didn't die of old age, Pilot. How do I know if it was natural or not? I'll tell you what killed him, and it will be up to you to figure out if somebody else arranged it."

"Fine. What killed him?"

"He suffocated. Note the cyanosis of the face, and the protruding tongue. See that little rash? Petechial hemorrhages."

"You mean somebody strangled him?"

"No, there's no evidence of that. Look at the swelling around the throat. You can see better from inside."

Pilot Barnes backed away. "I'll take your word."

"His throat is swollen up on the inside to the point that the trachea is completely blocked."

"What would do that?"

Dr. Putnam considered it. "A bee sting," he said thoughtfully. "If you happened to inhale one."

"There's your murderer," said Comfrey Stecoah triumphantly. "You going to arrest the bee?"

"I expect I'll find his body somewhere in their during the autopsy," said Dr. Putnam seriously. "One thing, though. Didn't you tell me that he was going for water when he was last seen?"

"That's right," said Jake. "Why?"

"There's traces of something in his mouth. Not water. I'm second-guessing the lab, but it smells to me like cider."

Milo turned to Jake. "Have we got any cider at the church? Did the day crew bring any in today?"

"No."

Dr. Putnam sighed. "All right, Pilot. Do your measuring and your picture taking. If it turns out to be cider in his mouth, and they didn't have cider with them, then I think somebody has committed a highly original murder."

"Not what I'd call a sure thing," said Comfrey. "I'd say it had more of a chance of failing than it did of succeeding."

"I don't know," said Jake. "Victor was allergic to bees."

"Who knew it?" asked Pilot Barnes.

Milo gave him a grim smile. "Who didn't?"

While Dr. Putnam finished his preliminary examination, Milo followed Pilot Barnes around the death scene, occasionally holding the camera or tape measure, and talking to the deputy in a low voice that Jake was unable to hear. After a few minutes, Jake saw him smile, pump Pilot's hand—disregarding the scowl he received in return—and walk back toward the church. Jake hurried to catch up with him.

He had intended to spend the walk back discussing the fate of the dig with Milo, but Comfrey Stecoah insisted on escorting them, making such a talk impossible. It was just as well, Jake told himself. Milo didn't seem to be in a talkative mood, despite his display of exuberance with the deputy. Even Victor's death did not account for depression of that magnitude. Jake concluded that the research was going badly.

"What are the chances of them solving this case?" Milo asked Comfrey after several hundred yards of silence.

Comfrey shrugged. "A little better than in New York. Same cop equipment, fewer suspects."

"Do you think somebody murdered Victor?" asked Jake.

"Maybe somebody crazy," said Milo. "They must have picked him because he was one of us and he happened to be the one they caught alone."

"Nothing personal, huh?" asked Jake, trying not to think of how close it had come to being Elizabeth out there alone.

"They're trying to keep you from helping us," Comfrey explained. "It's scare tactics. I wonder where Bevel Harkness was this morning."

"Well, if it was him, it will be safe to work out here tomorrow," Milo answered.

"Why?"

"Because the inquest on Alex is tomorrow. He has to testify."

"Is that what you were grinning at?" asked Jake.

"Back there with the deputy? No. I got him to agree to give us the skulls back tomorrow."

Elizabeth dabbed at her eyes. She had caught a glimpse of people in the woods about to emerge at the churchyard, and she didn't want to be caught crying, especially if one of those people turned out to be Milo. It was, she decided upon closer inspection. Should she avoid him or stay and find out what the matter was? I don't need this grief, she thought. Relationships are supposed to be pleasant. Ever since I got interested in Milo my life has turned into the waiting room of a dentist's office. She watched the three men draw nearer. Comfrey Stecoah said a few words to them and ambled off down the hillside toward the houses. Jake, seeing her on the porch, looked embarrassed. She nodded politely. With a murmured greeting, Jake brushed past her and disappeared inside the church. Milo stood looking down at her, tight-lipped. Elizabeth stared back unblinking.

"How are you?" asked Milo as if each word cost him.

"Fine," said Elizabeth, "considering that I discovered a body this afternoon."

"Well. I'm glad you're all right."

"Thank you," she answered primly.

Milo took a deep breath. Having got the preliminaries out of the way, he could say what was really on his mind. No one could say he hadn't been polite about it. "You screwed up the stats!" he burst out.

"I beg your pardon?"

"The skull measurements. I checked them today and they're all wrong."

"How could you check them when you don't have the skulls?"

"I compared them to the rest of the chart. They're way out of range. That must be what Alex wanted to tell me."

"Well, I'm not surprised, Milo. I kept asking you to check my work. I am a beginner, you know."

The perfect truth of what she said irritated him further. "Why couldn't you have been more careful?" he demanded. "You knew how important this was!"

Elizabeth glared at him. "If it was so important, perhaps you should have done a better job of supervising."

"Maybe I overestimated your intelligence!" Milo shot back.

Elizabeth looked away, her eyes stinging. I'll be damned if I let him see me cry, she thought. He is just upset about Alex's death. I ought to be more patient with him. Tapping the last dregs of Southern politeness, she managed a tight smile. "Would you like to show me the procedure again?"

Milo's frown relaxed. "We're getting the skulls back tomorrow, and since Mary Clare and Victor are not with us, I need to be doing other things. So I would *appreciate* it if you would do the measurements again!"

Under the circumstances, that speech would have to pass for an apology, Elizabeth decided. "Fine," she said, the arctic light still glinting in her eyes. "I'll do it again."

Milo, apparently finding the words "Thank you" unpronounceable, nodded and turned away.

CHAPTER FOURTEEN

DUMMYWEED squirmed uncomfortably in the patrol car, wishing he were a prisoner instead of a deputy. Prisoners got to make a phone call, had lawyers to get them out on bail. But since he was a shanghaied deputy with two murders to contend with, he didn't see a hope in hell of escaping the long arm of the law. He might not make it to the craft fair, and then Patricia would forget how much tax to charge, and things would be in complete chaos by the time he got back. He glared out the window, noticing for the first time that they were not on the road back to Laurel Cove.

"Where are we going?"

"We're going to pay a call on Bevel Harkness," said Pilot, his eyes on the road.

"Good. Once he takes over, you can give me a lift back to town." Over his protests, Dr. Putnam had been given the keys to Coltsfoot's car, and instructed to take the body back to town. Daniel hoped that this fact could be kept from Patricia; trading cars was such a hassle. He realized that Pilot had not responded to his request for a ride to town. "Or I could hitchhike," he added hopefully.

"'Fraid not," said Pilot. "Unless Harkness has an outstanding alibi which does not depend on members of his family, you are in it for the duration, son."

Coltsfoot sighed. He was afraid of that. "Is this Harkness guy a suspect, then?"

"Let's just say I'm taking no chances."

Coltsfoot played his last card. "I don't have any police training, you know."

"Uh-huh," nodded Pilot Barnes. "Well, you know those cop shows on the television? "Adam-12" and "Hawaii Five-0," that kind of thing?"

"Yeah, sure."

"Well, you forget everything you ever saw on them, and don't do nothing without I tell you to. You'll get along fine."

Coltsfoot slumped farther down in his seat, sighing. He wondered if they shot *deputies* for trying to escape.

Bevel Harkness lived in an old-style log house, gray logs wedged together with concrete, dating from the turn of the century. Its setting, with spreading oaks and wild mountain laurel, would have been impressive but for Harkness' unfortunate tendency to use the yard as a museum for old farm equipment.

Dummyweed, who drew the line at picturesque clutter, made a face. "Boy, what a slob!"

"Well," said Pilot mildly, "I don't know that it's all his fault. Seems like when the catalogue people started shipping civilization up here to the hills, they forgot to provide us with a modern garbage service. 'Course, some folks manage better than others."

Another thought struck the new deputy. "You're not going to arrest this guy, are you?"

"I'm aiming to question him. But if he confesses, I'll oblige. Let's go."

Pilot got out of the patrol car slowly, looking around. He didn't see anyone in the garden or near the house, so he headed for the front porch, ambling along as if he had no particular urgency in getting there. He waited until he saw an upstairs curtain stir before mounting the steps, motioning Dummyweed to follow. Two light taps on the door brought an unsmiling woman to answer it.

Pilot mopped his forehead, smiling politely.

"You're going to have to water that garden tonight," he remarked.

"Unless the clouds move in," the woman replied.

"Is Bevel around? I figured long as I was out this way, I'd stop in and see him." He sounded very casual. Pilot knew, and the woman knew, that the visit was official, but they kept to the ritual designed to see that no one panicked and no one got hurt.

"He's out in the pasture," the woman replied, her face still expressionless. "One of our cows dropped her calf today, and he went a-hunting it."

"Well, I reckon we'll walk on out there," said Pilot. "Might come across it while we're out looking for him. How long has he been at it?"

The woman hesitated. "An hour. Before that he was on patrol."

"Where 'bout?" asked Pilot, a shade too interested.

"Ask him," she shrugged, closing the door.

"What was that all about?" asked Dummyweed, when they were out of earshot.

"Well, he hasn't been home all day, which is what I needed to know. Now that I've got that, I can question him. You let me do the talking, though. One wrong word could cause more trouble than we're equipped to handle."

Dummyweed turned pale. "You think he'd shoot us?" he hissed.

"Coltsfoot, if he's killed two people, I don't reckon he'd faint at the thought of killing four."

After this unwelcome pronouncement, Dummyweed lapsed into silence, spending the rest of the walk scouring the hills for smoke signals, machine gun nests—he knew not what. They found Bevel Harkness past the pond and up the side of the hill, searching through bushes for the missing cow. He scowled at them warily, sensing the magnitude of trouble that would bring them out there.

"What is it?" he growled.

185

"You mind telling me what you did today?" asked Pilot, carefully polite.

"Did my rounds. Why?"

"Anybody see you?"

"Now and then. It was too hot out there for most folks. You want to tell me what this is all about?"

"Directly," nodded Pilot. "Would you have any objection to coming down to the office and having your fingerprints taken?"

Harkness' eyes narrowed. "I believe I would."

"Well, I'm sorry to hear that," said Pilot apologetically. "Because you give me no choice but to suspend you for the course of this investigation. Two murders in Sarvice Valley related to this strip-mining business is more than I can overlook. Unless, of course, you'd agree to a polygraph, or—"

"Get off my land," said Harkness in the softest of voices.

"On our way!" Dummyweed blurted out. "Have a nice day!"

When they reached the patrol car, Dummyweed asked: "What are you going to do now that you didn't get his fingerprints?"

Pilot smiled. "Get 'em off his coffee cup at the office."

"Then why did you come out here and ask for them?"

"I couldn't lay him off without an excuse, could I?" He maneuvered the car down the driveway. "You see, Coltsfoot, the sheriff doesn't much like the Harknesses, especially since his nephew disappeared about ten years ago after taking on the deputy job in Sarvice Valley. That job had kinda been in their family awhile, and it looked mighty suspicious when Carver Johnson disappeared two weeks after replacing a Harkness."

"What did they do to him?" asked Coltsfoot hoarsely, realizing who the present Sarvice Valley replacement was.

"Never found him," grunted Pilot. "No evidence against them. But now that we have two fresh bodies in a situation that Harkess is mixed up in, why, I'll see if I can't find a connection."

"He just disappeared?" murmured Coltsfoot, still thinking of the last non-Cullowhee deputy.

"Without a trace," said Pilot Barnes solemnly. Catching sight of Dummyweed's green and anxious face, it was all he could do not to laugh.

"You don't suppose they'd mind my having skulls in the church do you?" asked Elizabeth, peering into the box.

Jake shrugged. "They were all members, probably."

"I guess. It was nice of Mr. Barnes to bring them back this morning, wasn't it? Do you think we should have gone to the inquest?"

"Nope. It's just a formality, anyway. They're going to announce that Alex died of a blow to the head, and that it was done by some person unknown. We already know that. I think it's enough that Milo is representing our group."

"You're right." Elizabeth unwrapped the measuring tools.

"Besides, you'll have to go to the inquest on Victor since you found the body. You might as well stay and get some work done while you can."

"Don't you think someone ought to be with Milo?"

Jake sighed. "I think we ought to leave him alone for a while. I get the feeling that he's alone even when he's here."

"He wants to finish the project. For Alex. I wish I hadn't made a mess of it."

Jake stared at her. "Will you snap out of it? You put him behind by maybe one day. That's not such a big deal. On my first dig, I troweled through three soil layers, two black and one red clay, without noticing the difference."

Elizabeth smiled. "Are you going to stay up here while I work?" She had decided to stay in the common room to do the measurements so that there would be no distractions from heat or insects.

"I'm not going up to the site alone," he replied. "In fact, I wish I had told the day crew to come back today. I don't feel very safe out here with just the two of us."

"Yes," said Elizabeth absently, intent upon her measuring. "Especially if I find who I'm looking for here."

Jake nodded, glancing down at his book. A few moments later, her words set off an alarm in his mind. "What did you say?"

"Hmm? Nothing. Don't distract me." Elizabeth scribbled down a number in her notebook.

"No, wait a minute. What was that about 'if I find who I'm looking for'?"

"I'm not supposed to tell," said Elizabeth in a small voice.

"Look, if you know something that's going to get both of us killed, the least you could do is let me in on it!"

Elizabeth looked around nervously, expecting to see faces leering at them from the windows. "We'll be fine," she said nervously. "Everybody is at the inquest."

"Which adjourns in about five minutes," said Jake, consulting his watch.

"All right," she sighed. "I guess I can trust you."

Jake laughed. "Considering that you are alone in this church with me in the middle of nowhere, you might as well."

"Don't!" Elizabeth shivered. "I don't want to think about it." She put the skull back in the box. "Milo thinks one of these skulls is a ringer."

"One of them isn't a Cullowhee?"

"That's what we think. Remember that story you told me about the Moonshine Massacre, and how the sheriff's nephew disappeared?" Her voice sank to a whisper. "What if it's him?"

"Of course! What better place to hide a murder victim than in with a bunch of old bones?"

Elizabeth nodded. "That's what we figured. But so far I haven't been able to prove it."

"So far they're all Cullowhees, huh?"

"Oh, Jake, I don't know!" wailed Elizabeth. "I messed up all the measurements the first time, and now this one has come out the same as before!"

"I'm distracting you," said Jake quickly. "No wonder you can't concentrate. Now, don't cry! I'll just sit here and read, and you start over. Okay?"

"Okay," said Elizabeth, wiping her eyes.

The next hour passed in silence. Jake settled back with his book, occasionally peeping over the top of it at Elizabeth. She was intent upon her work: measuring, writing down the result, shaking her head, and measuring again. Finally he could stand it no longer. "How's it going? You look worried."

She shook her head. "It doesn't make any sense."

"Did you find the ringer? It isn't that tiny one, is it?"

"No. I've been concentrating on the skull measurements, and I don't understand it. I came out with the same numbers I got the first time."

"So?"

"Milo says they're all wrong. They don't fit the chart."

"Have you checked your instruments?" asked Jake thoughtfully.

"No. I wouldn't know how to go about it. Do you think something is wrong with them?"

"It's possible, isn't it? If somebody put your tools out of alignment, you're not going to get any helpful results, are you?"

"I guess not. I'll ask Milo if— Did you hear a car?"

Jake peered out the window. "It isn't Milo. It's the sheriff's car."

"Milo isn't here," Elizabeth told the deputy.

"No, I know he isn't. I left him back in town," Pilot told her. "Like you to meet Ron Garrett, FBI agent. He's helping us on the case." He turned to Jake. "We'd like to talk to you."

Elizabeth's stomach lurched. Surely not Jake, she thought. A moment later she found she didn't believe it. "Would you like me to leave?" she asked Jake. "Shall I call Milo?"

"No, it's okay. What would you like to know, gentlemen?"

"Is your name Jake Adair?" asked Pilot, consulting a printed card.

"Yep," said Jake calmly. He didn't seem surprised at being questioned.

"And your home is in Swain County, North Carolina."

"Right. Route 1, Box 109, Cherokee."

Pilot eyed him sternly. "That is the Cherokee Indian reservation, ain't it?"

"It sure is," Jake agreed cheerfully.

"That's neat!" exclaimed Elizabeth, forgetting the interrogation. "How did you come to live there?"

"Because I'm a full-blooded Cherokee," said Jake, smiling gently.

"But—you—but . . ." Elizabeth realized that all the things she had been about to say were equally stupid, so she hushed and mulled over this turn of events while the officers resumed their questioning.

"Are you aware of the weapon used to kill Dr. Alex Lerche?" the deputy demanded.

"A tomahawk," said Jake wearily.

"A souvenir tomahawk from the Cherokee reservation," Garrett corrected him.

"Those things are shipped over by the carload

190

from Taiwan. Shouldn't you be questioning Chinese suspects, sir?"

"Have you ever had such a weapon in your possession?" barked Pilot, ignoring this sally.

"Not since I was eight years old."

"Do you have any objection to having your fingerprints taken?"

"Help yourself."

"This is silly!" cried Elizabeth. "Why should he kill Alex? The Cherokees have nothing to do with all this!"

Jake smiled. "Well, I'd say this was our land about six hundred years ago, but I'm not here to foreclose on it."

The officers were not amused. "Is there any way the Cherokees could get this land back?" Pilot murmured to the FBI agent.

"About the same odds as you winning the Irish Sweepstakes," said Jake cheerfully.

"Have you connected him to the tomahawk?" Elizabeth demanded.

Pilot looked pained. "Ma'am, unless you are his attorney of record, would you please stay out of this?"

Elizabeth scowled. "My brother is in law school."

"It's all right," said Jake soothingly. "These gentlemen just want my fingerprints because they're being thorough. You aren't going to haul me away in handcuffs, are you?"

Pilot Barnes and Ron Garrett exchanged exasperated glances. They had expected their surprise questioning to elicit frightened cooperation, but it wasn't working. Garrett shrugged. "We'll take your prints, run them through our computer, and see what we get. Don't plan on going anywhere."

After a few more minutes' questioning, the officers took Jake's fingerprints and left. When the door closed behind them, Elizabeth put the last skull back in the box and smiled up at Jake. "Hey, can I measure your jawline?"

Jake laughed. "You didn't know, did you? Out at the site when you told me I looked like an Apache, I thought you must have guessed."

Elizabeth shook her head. "You don't ... uh ... you're not what I expected."

"No long hair and feathers, huh? Sorry to disappoint you. The coroner knew, though, the first time he saw me."

"How?"

"He asked if I was a Cullowhee, and when I said no, he wanted to know my last name. I told him Adair, and he said: 'So that's it!' Adair is a very famous Cherokee name."

"Why didn't you tell us?"

Jake smiled. "Dr. Lerche knew. So did Milo. But I don't usually broadcast it. I get tired of the dumb questions: 'Do you live in a tepee?' And the stale jokes: 'How! You see, I speak your language.' I didn't want to hear any more of it."

Elizabeth nodded. "Like Victor, saying his great-grandmother was a Cherokee princess."

"Oh, God," groaned Jake. "That one is the worst. All of you *unakas* claim your grandmother was a Cherokee. Why can't you pick on the Shawnee? And why is it always a great-grandmother?"

Elizabeth frowned. "What was that word you used?"

"*Unaka?* That's the Cherokee word for honky. Understand, I'm proud of my heritage. I just get tired of people getting so hung up with it that they can't see *me.*"

"What?" murmured Elizabeth. She didn't seem to be listening.

"What's the matter with you?"

Elizabeth blinked. "Sorry. I guess it's the heat. I was wondering what we were going to have for lunch."

"And I thought you were getting nervous about being here with me," Jake grumbled.

"No. I know you didn't do it," she replied.

"Well, thanks for the vote of confidence."

But it isn't a matter of faith, she thought, it's just that I know who did it. Now how am I going to get rid of you so that I can find out why? Elizabeth assumed her most simpering smile, the one usually reserved for flat tires on interstates. "Jake, do you think you could go to Comfrey's house and get some tomatoes from his garden? He said we could help ourselves, and I want to make tomato sandwiches for lunch."

"Why don't we both go?" asked Jake, getting up.

"Okay," said Elizabeth.

When they reached the door, she stopped, as if something had just occurred to her. "You know, we're almost out of iced tea. Why don't I stay here and make some while you're getting the tomatoes. You won't be gone long, will you?" She asked anxiously.

"Ten or fifteen minutes," said Jake. "Don't let anybody in while I'm gone, okay?"

"I promise," said Elizabeth solemnly. She stood on the porch and watched him walk out of sight. A moment later she was gone.

CHAPTER FIFTEEN

PILOT BARNES slowed down to let a groundhog scuttle across the road. Had it appeared in his garden, he would have shot it without a qualm; the incongruity of this never struck him. "What did you think of that interview?" he asked the FBI agent.

"The Adair kid?" Garrett shook his head. "I don't buy it. Remember at the time of the second murder, he didn't leave the work site. That gives him a lot of witnesses for an alibi; but there's still a chance he may know something. Our check on him didn't turn up anything unusual."

"He's an Indian," grunted Pilot.

"Oh, that's no big deal. My great-grandmother was a Cherokee. That's where I got my brown eyes. I still say he's off the hook. In fact, those two might be in danger. Have you thought about putting a guard out there?"

"I don't think they need one."

"Better play it safe," Garrett advised.

The deputy smiled. "Tell you what: I'll compromise. I'll send Dummyweed out to guard them."

"Symbolic deterrent, huh? Might work. That will free you and McKenna to check up on the other people. Are any of the suspects from the first murder out of the picture now? What about the wife?"

"Nope. You saw her at the inquest, didn't you? She got in last night."

"She's a possibility. Could have killed the husband and been seen by this Bassington fellow. Blackmail?"

Pilot thought it over. "Can we get a record of long-distance calls to her house? Or maybe get the Virginia police to search her place for blackmailing letters?"

"I'll see what I can do," said Garrett. "Anything else?"

"The girlfriend. She was out walking when the first murder took place, and right after that she left to do research at MacDowell."

"So?"

"Yesterday she came back to get her guitar. Makes me wonder why she left it in the first place."

"Check up on her, too," sighed the agent. "You're lucky we don't charge you locals for computer time."

Pilot felt the discomfort of obligation. "I'm mighty grateful to you for helping me out like this," he said awkwardly.

"No problem, Deputy. You sure are putting in a lot of overtime on this case. Personal interest?"

Pilot shook his head. "I just want to clear it up before the sheriff gets back." To show him what I can do without supervision, he finished silently. He can't stay sheriff forever; maybe there *is* a promotion in this. He didn't think it was going to happen, though. Pilot Barnes couldn't shake the feeling that he was missing some vital thread of the investigation, something that he might not even recognize if it were put before him. Duncan Johnson, he told himself, would have caught it in a minute. Pilot Barnes stared morosely at the Wise Woman of the Woods sign; it didn't take a prophet to tell him he didn't have a hope in hell of becoming sheriff.

Tessa Lerche, forewarned that the inquest would take place in an un-air-conditioned courtroom, did not wear black. In her beige linen suit, matching bone shoes, and touches of gold jewelry at the ears and throat, she seemed a cool and neutral observer to the proceedings inquiring into her husband's death. In fact, she would not wear black at all except to the funeral; it seemed hypocritical in one who had lately been studying pamphlets on community property in divorce, and Tessa loathed the semblance of hyprocrisy. She gave her evidence of accompanying Milo to the site on the night of the murder, speaking in a clear, calm voice softened by sorrow. She had used such a voice once in a college production of *Riders to the Sea*, in the old woman's speech: "They're all gone now, and there's nothing more the sea can do to me ..." Traces of a brogue crept into her testimony, causing the more astute listeners to suppose her Irish by birth.

Stepping down from the witness stand, she took her seat beside Milo and listened to the medical evidence with the blank face of one whose thoughts were elsewhere. Once, at some particularly graphic phrase uttered by the coroner, Milo glanced at her, but she looked up at him with a half-smile and continued to study the placement of her neat little hands, clutching the calfskin purse in her lap.

When the verdict "murder by person or persons unknown" had been delivered, he escorted her outside, protectively watching for reporters with cameras, but none appeared. (Stuart Morton, editor of the *Recorder*, was off covering the 4-H camp. He would give the inquest the customary six lines on page three.)

"Thank you for seeing me through this," said Tessa softly. "It meant a lot."

Milo shifted nervously. "Are you driving back now?"

She looked up at him with moist eyes. "Will you think it terrible of me if I tell you I'd like to have lunch first? I guess I should get used to eating alone, but ..." She trailed off, a quaver in her voice.

"Of course," said Milo, wondering how she had managed to make him feel guilty. "Where would you like to go?"

Tessa sighed. "It doesn't matter. I never notice

what I eat any more. Only I couldn't bear to be on public display in some local café." She shuddered delicately.

After some discussion it was decided that the Rhododendron Inn, an Edwardian mansion outfitted as a tavern, would suit Tessa's sense of propriety. Milo, checking his hip pocket for his credit card, agreed without noticeable enthusiasm. The Rhododendron Inn, half-timbered and decorated with farm implements on the walls, fancied itself the sort of place where George Washington might have dined, had he been willing to mortgage Mount Vernon to pay for the meal.

When they had been seated at a small pine table with a mason jar of wildflowers between them, Tessa whispered, "I hope they don't serve that greasy country food!"

Milo, who hoped they did, said, "Why don't you order a salad?"

Milo opted for the country buffet, leaving Tessa to quiche du jour and pumpkin muffins. He stayed in the buffet line longer than he might have had he been anxious to return to his table partner. He wondered if Tessa merely wanted to rehash the inquest or if she had something else in mind.

"How do you think it went?" she asked him, trying not to look at the steaming plate of pinto beans and fried apples.

"The inquest? Pretty routine, I guess."

"I can't help feeling that the police have someone in mind as a suspect, but that they don't want to show their hand yet."

"I doubt it," said Milo between mouthfuls. "Since there has been another murder, I expect they'd arrest somebody if they could."

"Poor ... Victor," Tessa responded, trying to remember if she'd met him. "I suppose he must have seen something?"

"I don't know. Even if he did, it's hard to imagine

197

any of us believing him. Victor was such a liar he'd have said anything. We all ignored him."

She shook her head reprovingly, as if to remind him not to speak ill of the dead. "Still, he will be missed. Have you told his family yet?"

"I called them this morning," said Milo sharply, unwilling to discuss it further. Victor's mother had succumbed to hysterics as if on cue, but his father had been gravely calm. He seemed to regard the episode as Victor's most ambitious bid for attention.

"Even the most inconsiderate, self-centered people are mourned by those who loved them," sighed Tessa. She managed to imply that this was the case with Alex.

When Milo, in what she supposed to be an excess of sympathy for her past and present suffering, did not reply to this, Tessa tried again: "I suppose you'll be coming back to town soon?"

"Probably tomorrow. Depends on what arrangements are being made about Victor."

Tessa had a sudden image of Milo conveying Victor's body home to Maryland in a station wagon; she was sure that this was not what he meant, but since she wasn't interested in the details anyway, she let it pass. "You will come and see me when you get back, won't you?"

"Of course. I thought you'd want me to take charge of Alex's papers."

"That, too," murmured Tessa.

Milo raised his head, like one who has just heard ticking from the luggage rack above him. "Too?"

"Oh, Milo, there are just so many things to cope with now that Alex is gone! You know, taxes, and the will . . ."

"Didn't he have a lawyer?"

"Yes, but . . . And I have to dispose of his clothes."

"Goodwill box, corner of Elm and Sycamore."

"You don't understand," said Tessa in an exasperated voice. "I just can't seem to cope with this ... this ..."

"I believe the Crisis Center has a seminar on coping with bereavement," said Milo evenly. "I'm sure they could help you more than I."

She pursed her lips. "I'm sure I'll feel much better when they've arrested that cat-faced little colleague of yours! She meant to get Alex one way or another, and the police know it, too!"

A diffident figure in khaki approached their table. Milo was never so glad to see anyone in his life. Bewildered at the effusiveness of the greeting, Dummyweed blinked at them, surprised that the fellow who had always been curt with him should have taken such a liking to him now. Perhaps it was the new uniform; one of Pilot's, actually, but it fit well enough.

"I saw your car outside," he told them. "Mr. Barnes wants me to go back to Sarvice Valley on guard duty."

Under any other circumstances, Milo would have told him to get lost, but now that he presented an alternative to prolonging the interview with Tessa, Milo was the soul of cooperation. "Of course!" he said, getting up. "Do you need me to come with you? Does Barnes need to see me?"

"No. I need a ride." Seeing their startled faces, Coltsfoot hastened to explain. "See, we only have two patrol cars. Mr. McKenna needs one to patrol the county, and Pilot's using the other one over at the Nunwati Nature-Friends Craft Fair, which is tonight." He paused on a wistful note, but no expressions of sympathy were forthcoming.

"What about Harkness' car?"

"Oh, he just used his own, and they paid him mileage. County figured it was cheaper."

"Couldn't you take your own car?"

"Patricia won't let me have it," murmured Coltsfoot, reddening. "I was wondering if you'd mind me

199

riding out with you. I don't know why Pilot didn't run me out there when he went. Maybe he hadn't decided they needed me then. I was setting up for the craft fair when they came and got me."

Milo cut him off. "Barnes has been to Sarvice Valley since the inquest? What for?"

"I don't know. I think he was questioning somebody. He had the FBI guy with him."

Milo turned to Tessa. "Would you like me to drop you back at the courthouse? I think I should go back now."

Tessa, who had just remembered what it was like to live with a dedicated scientist, managed a brave smile. "No thanks, Milo. I'll make it on my own."

Daniel Hunter Coltsfoot spent most of the ride to Sarvice Valley complaining about the circumstances that had led to his becoming a deputy. Patricia Elf needn't complain now about having to set the booths up by herself at the craft fair; if it weren't for her, he wouldn't be in this mess.

"And I'd say that the Sarvice Valley killer is a lot more likely to get *me* than those Tennessee convicts were to get *her* when she insisted I buy that gun!" he finished bitterly.

"Why don't you just refuse to do it?" asked Milo. "Sense of duty?"

"Of course. I *am* a deputy," said Coltsfoot with a noble lift of his chin. "And besides, Pilot happened to mention that if I didn't go through with it until this investigation is over, he was going to get a lot more interested in minor drug offenses in the county."

"I see," said Milo, stifling a smile.

"Damn right. The Nature-Friends would *kill* me."

"I see you brought a gun," Milo remarked, glancing at the holster on Dummyweed's belt. "Do you know how to use it?"

"I've never tried, but it looks easy enough on television. Bang, bang, you're dead. Right, man?"

"Oh, boy," said Milo to himself.

"I'm strictly nonviolent myself. Peace marches; run for hunger; demonstrations against the nuclear power plants." He slapped the pistol on his thigh. "But when there's a killer out there and you're the law—a man's gotta do what he's gotta do."

"Right," said Milo, turning at a cluster of houses. "I think I'll stop and get Comfrey Stecoah. You wait here."

He hurried up the concrete steps and tapped on the door. In a moment, Comfrey Stecoah himself appeared and ushered Milo into a small, sparse living room. Comfrey, still wearing the clothes he had on at the inquest, had been eating his lunch on the chrome and glass coffee table.

"What is it?" he asked Milo.

"Pilot Barnes assigned us a guard for the rest of our stay."

"'Bout time," grunted Comfrey.

"It's that Coltsfoot guy. With a gun." Milo enunciated each word carefully, underscoring the implications.

"Right. Let me finish eating. I'll meet you at the church."

He's a good guy, Milo thought as he walked back to the car. If they fire Bevel Harkness, they ought to hire him as deputy in the valley. Maybe I'll mention it to Pilot Barnes.

"How much longer are you guys going to be here?" asked Coltsfoot when they were on their way again.

"We should be gone by tomorrow, I hope," said Milo. "We're remeasuring the skulls today, and then we'll rebury the remains. I can do the computer work back at the university. Two days, at the most."

"I'll still miss the craft fair," sighed Coltsfoot.

. Milo pulled the car into the parking lot below the

church. Before he got halfway up the bank, Jake came running to meet them.

"Have you seen Elizabeth?" he demanded.

Milo's eyes narrowed. "I left her here with you!"

"She sent me out for tomatoes," said Jake sheepishly. "When I came back, she was gone!"

Elizabeth was in no hurry to get where she was going. She needed the time to think. By the time she reached the path up the mountain, Elizabeth was sure that she had not been followed. She had at least ten minutes' head start before Jake came back and began to search for her. By the time he found her, she hoped she would have everything settled. She slowed to a walk, forcing herself to look at the plants along the path, while her mind considered the problem. Bloodroot and yarrow ... could she ever tell Milo the truth? Boneset ... pigweed ... maybe she could have brought Jake with her. He might have understood. Could he track her through the woods? She frowned. Of course he couldn't! Indian stereotyping again.

She stooped to examine a yellow-orange tangle of vines in a sunny spot beside the path—the love vine. She had found it in her plant book under "dodder—also known as strangleweed." She wondered if anyone had planted this one, and if so whose name it bore. A cluster of gnats swarmed up into her face, and she batted them away. The air was thick with heat.

"Think this through," Elizabeth said aloud wishing for a moment that she could turn and go back to the church. Whose responsibility was it anyway? She had nearly reached the end of the path—not far now. Soon Milo would figure out what she already knew, and by then it would be too late to salvage anything from the confusion that would follow. Elizabeth kept going. She had to talk to the Wise Woman of the Woods.

Amelanchier's cabin sat in green silence in the clearing. Elizabeth was relieved to see that no tourists had made the trek up the mountain. She stood in the shadow of a sourwood tree, watching a red-tailed hawk on a reconnaissance flight. It flew a back loop toward a thatch of pines, out of her line of sight. She wondered if she ought to search for Amelanchier, perhaps at the creek whose wind-sound barely reached her ears. She looked again at the still cabin, deep in shade; its doors and windows faced her like a blank stare. *She knows I am here*, thought Elizabeth. *She sees me.* She wondered how she knew.

As Elizabeth turned over her feelings, she was surprised to find that her reluctance to go on came from shyness rather than from fear. Elizabeth was never very direct with anyone. "Are you going to the kitchen?" she would say to Bill—*not*, "Bring me a glass of water." She wondered if there were any diplomatic way to discuss multiple murder, but she was not afraid. Never once did she think: I could be next.

She walked slowly through the fescue grass, knowing that she was not within the cross hairs of a rifle sight, not bothering to move in stealth. She would not ring the yard bell or "rad" a note; and she must not think of Victor or Alex for the next half hour.

Elizabeth tapped on the door.

"It's open!" Amelanchier's voice sang out.

Elizabeth eased the door open and peered inside. The old woman sat at her plank worktable, scooping dried herbs into small plastic bags. "Making up a batch of bitters," she told Elizabeth. "Tourists cleaned me out."

She motioned her visitor toward the stool against the wall. "You want to tie them tags around the neck of the bags for me?" she asked, shoving a handful of garbage-bag ties across the table.

203

Elizabeth picked up the wire and plastic sealer and began to wind it around the neck of the bitters packet. "We have to talk," she said softly.

"Makes the time pass more pleasant-like when you do," Amelanchier agreed.

"I don't think it will this time, Amelanchier, but it's got to be done. Just remember, I'm here to help you."

"And I'm grateful to you," said the Wise Woman cheerfully. "Sure is a raft of these bags to tie."

"No, I mean about saving the valley. I don't want the Cullowhees to lose it to the strip miners. Especially after what I've heard about what your people have been through already. It wouldn't be fair!"

Amelanchier nodded and went on stuffing plastic bags.

"You have to confess to the murders, Amelanchier," said Elizabeth quietly. "And we have to come up with some excuse for why you did it, because if the truth comes out, you'll lose the valley!"

"What truth is that?"

"The Cullowhees aren't Indians."

Amelanchier smiled. "Why, sure we are girl. It's like I told you: we're descended from the Unakas—"

"Yes! And *unaka* is the Cherokee word for white man! Now who are you really?"

Amelanchier wiped her hands on her apron. "Well," she sighed, "I think you said something about saving the valley. Why don't I brew us some tea and we'll study about it?"

She drew out earthenware mugs and plastic spoons. "Now how can you tell what people is?" she asked as she worked. "That word don't prove nothing."

"You know how I can tell. I explained it to you the first time I came up here. I told you all about the skull measurements, and how different races show up as different numbers on the chart."

"I thought the doctor was the only one could say for sure."

"Dr. Lerche could tell just by looking at a skull. The rest of us don't have his experience, so we have to plod along with charts, but we'll get there. I did the measurements twice, and they don't match the rest of the chart. When Milo checks my work and sees that I did it right, he'll know, too. Then the secret will be out,`and we don't want that."

"What about saving the valley?"

"If the investigation continues, the secret will come out. But if you confess, and if I fake the report, then everyone will get the answers they want, and that will be the end of it."

"So we both tell lies?" smiled Amelanchier.

"Yes. Except for the fact that you killed Dr. Lerche and Victor. That's true."

The old woman looked as if she was going to deny it, but suddenly she sighed wearily and asked, "How come you to know?"

"Because it's my fault!" said Elizabeth, close to tears. "I realized that it couldn't have been Comfrey, because if he had known that the Cullowhees weren't Indians, he wouldn't have come asking for scientific proof. And you knew all about this project from me. You even knew that Victor was allergic to bees, because I told you! I even told you that he bragged about knowing who killed Alex, but I forgot to tell you what a liar he was! I don't think he knew anything, really."

"Well, I couldn't take the chance. My people have had it too hard to risk losing everything to some no-account college boy. I reckon you want your tea sweet, don't you? It'll have to be honey. I don't keep the white sugar. It'll do you in."

Elizabeth picked up her steaming mug and took a sip. It still tasted bitter, even with honey in it. "Who are you really? Does anybody know?"

"Only me. I'm the oldest one alive, so I remember

when folks knew. My grandfather still had the whip scars on his back."

"You were slaves then? Run away from plantations?"

"Sold from the plantations," said Amelanchier in a steady voice. "Run away from the Cherokees."

Elizabeth's eyes widened. "The Cherokees? That's impossible! They were an Indian tribe."

"I reckon you think Indians is somebody who lives in a tepee and wears war paint and feathers," Amelanchier snorted. "Well, I can't speak for the ones out west, but I'm here to tell you that them Cherokees turned white faster than ash wood in a bonfire."

"They owned slaves?"

"Yes, ma'am, and had big old farms to work 'em on. Took white last names, and got religion around 1800. Started intermarrying with the whites, too. I reckon they figured that if they got civilized, the white folks would let 'em be."

"Did it work?" Elizabeth was hazy on Appalachian history, which wasn't taught until fall semester.

"It did not. The Cherokee nation was good land, timber and gold, and good acres for farming. About 1830, when the settlers started running out of room on the coast, they commenced nagging the government to get the Indians off the good land, move 'em farther west."

"The Trail of Tears," whispered Elizabeth, suddenly remembering.

"Yep. Kicked right out, just like they want to do to us. All except five hundred who hid in the hills. It's their descendants who have the Cherokee reservation today."

"And were the slaves freed when the Indians were forced to move?"

"No, they were moved right on out with the cattle. But my people didn't go. They run off and came back to the hills. Been here ever since. Most of 'em was half-breeds, mixed black and white."

"And Indian?"

"I don't believe so. They used to say that the Indians gave fifty lashes to any of their tribe who married a slave."

"But why did you claim to be Indian?" asked Elizabeth, shuddering as she sipped her tea.

"Because between 1830 and very recently, being anything else was not healthy around here. If they'd said they were black, they could'a been took back in slavery till the War between the States, and even after that they was worse off than the Indians. At least we never had no lynchings to worry about."

"But everyone knew you weren't really Indian?"

Amelanchier nodded. "It was my gran'daddy, the Wise Man, who changed that. When I was a little bitty girl, he told folks that the best way to keep a secret is not to tell it out, so from then on, the children were told they was real Indians. When I go, the truth goes with me; I never told a one of my young'uns any different. I never knowed you could tell from the bones of the dead."

"Not until I told you," said Elizabeth. She mustn't think about that now; she mustn't! "I don't want your people to lose the land. It isn't fair."

"I wish Comfrey would have told me before he asked you'uns to come here. But he thinks I'm an old woman who don't know nothing but plants."

"It can't be helped," said Elizabeth briskly. She wondered how much time they had before Jake found her. "We have to figure out some reason other than the truth for you to have killed them! How about this: you killed them because you didn't want the bones of your relatives disturbed by irreverent white scientists?"

"I was thinking of that myself," said Amelanchier. "More tea?"

CHAPTER SIXTEEN

"WHAT DO YOU MEAN she's gone?" Milo demanded. "Did she leave a note?"

"No. I thought she must have gone down to the creek or something, but I've called and she doesn't answer."

"Have you checked the site?" asked Milo. He couldn't think of any reason for her to go there, but it was the only possibility that occurred to him.

"No. Shall we go out there now?"

"In a minute. Comfrey Stecoah is coming along. What happened here that would make Elizabeth leave? What did the deputy want?"

"He found out I'm a Cherokee, and he wanted to see if he could scare me into a confession. On account of the tomahawk."

Milo considered this piece of information. "Was Elizabeth frightened?" he asked finally.

"If you mean, did she think I was going to scalp her, I don't think so."

"Well, what was she doing?"

"She spent most of the morning remeasuring those skulls. That, and moping about how nasty you've been lately."

Milo's lips tightened. "I have not been nasty! I've been professional. Those measurements had to be done correctly, whether it hurt her feelings or not."

Jake scowled back. "Yeah? Well, suppose she did them correctly in the first place?"

"I wish she had," said Milo softly.

"Maybe she did," said Dummyweed brightly. He had no idea what they were talking about, but he felt

208

that as representative of the law, it was time to say something, and that seemed appropriate.

It seemed to make sense to Jake. "Yeah," he said evenly. "Maybe she did."

Milo, who had never considered that possibility, was shaken. "What do you mean?"

"I sat here and watched her do those figures again for a couple of hours, man," Jake informed him. "And she was getting the exact same answers she got the first time."

"That's impossible!"

"Why?" asked Dummyweed, interested.

They ignored him.

"The numbers don't fit the chart," said Milo, as if that settled it.

"Okay," nodded Jake. "Assume for a moment that Elizabeth's figures are right. That leaves two choices. One: that Alex faked or screwed up ten years of research on Plains Indians, or two . . ."

"That the Cullowhees are not Indians," said Milo faintly.

"Take your pick," shrugged Jake.

"Let me see those skulls!"

When Comfrey Stecoah found them in the common room some ten minutes later, Milo had measured two of the skulls, and his face looked as much of a death's-head as any of them. Jake and the deputy were kneeling beside the crate, looking equally grim.

"Where's the young lady?" asked Comfrey, looking around.

"You tell us!" Jake shot back.

"Elizabeth is missing," Milo said as calmly as he could. "We're going to check the site for her. Would you come with us, please?"

Comfrey shook his head, presumably at the strangeness of the female sex. "What made her take off?" he wondered aloud.

"I think it was a discovery she made this morning,

209

Mr. Stecoah. According to the tests she did"—he paused for effect—"the Cullowhees are not Indian!"

"Oh, is that all?" said Comfrey. "Shoot far, I could'a told you that."

Milo, to whom live people were always a closed book—of hieroglyphics—thought he had gone mad. Surely he could not have just heard ... "What did you say?"

"I figured it out for myself when I was doing research into the origin stories. That's how I spotted you, Little Beaver," he said, nodding at Jake.

"Don't call me—"

"Reckon we belonged to your gang a long time back. But all the other folks around here still believe they're Indians, and I never told 'em no different."

"But why did you call us in to do the study if you already knew?" Milo's head was spinning.

"Oh, for the government, son. To make it look good. We filed a formal request for recognition with the Bureau of Indian Affairs, and we had to send a list of things we were doing to substantiate our claim. Old maps, birth certificates showing residence in this county. I figured a scientific study would look real official."

"But it would disprove your case," said Milo patiently.

"Oh, shoot, that didn't worry me! You don't understand the government. I know you fellows always tack words like 'probably' and 'generally' into your reports. You never say anything flat out simple. Most folks don't read all those technical reports nohow, and them that do may not believe 'em. The report would look good in our case file, though."

"But we'll have to say that you aren't Indian, and they won't give you the land." Another thought struck him. "Who are you, anyway?"

"Well, judging from what I found out, I'd say we were escaped slaves from the Cherokee nation. We got a family of Rosses up on the ridge; that's a Cherokee last name."

"So's Stecoah," murmured Jake.

"Is that possible?" asked Milo, turning to Jake.

"Sure. The Cherokees were the biggest slaveholders of any of the five nations. Bought 'em from the settlers."

"Didn't marry any, though," said Comfrey.

"Usually not," Jake admitted.

Milo shook his head incredulously. "So you're a mixture of blacks and Anglo-Saxons. No wonder you didn't fit the chart! And all this was for nothing, because you won't get the land."

Comfrey smiled easily. "Oh, I think we will. Don't you, Little Beaver?"

Jake scowled. "Probably."

"How can they give you a reservation when you're not Indians?" asked Milo.

"I expect the other tribes will insist on letting us in," Comfrey told him. "Otherwise, it might be bad for them in the long run."

"This makes absolutely no sense!"

"Yes, it does," Jake assured him.

"It's politics," explained the leader of the Cullowhees. "You see, if they kept us from getting tribal recognition, what would their grounds be?"

"That you aren't Indian."

"Racial impurity," Comfrey corrected him. "That we are not pure-bred. But we *do* have a group identity, and we *do* claim to be Indian, and have claimed it for years."

"So?"

"So if we get disqualified on the grounds of racial impurity, that will make all the other Indian tribes mighty damn nervous."

"Why?" asked Milo, fascinated.

"Because who *is* pure nowadays? The Navajos are mixed with Hispanics, like most of the rest of the bunch out west—"

"And the Cherokees started marrying white settlers in 1809," murmured Jake.

"I didn't think Adair sounded very Indian," Milo admitted.

"Yep. If they started kicking out impure Indians, they'd have to start worrying about who'd be next. Maybe someday uranium would be discovered on the old reservation, and bingo! Uncle Sam would decide that your tribe wasn't pure enough to deserve the land. Yep, they wouldn't like to see *that* precedent set. Not over one little old valley in the Smokies. We've made enough noise about being Indian to where we'd embarrass every tribe in the country if they kicked us out now."

"That's very clever," said Dummyweed.

"Just politics," said Comfrey modestly.

"Why was Alex killed?" asked Milo quietly. He was sure it was tied in to all this.

"I don't know," said Comfrey. "Unless the strip miners did it, figuring he'd prove we were the real thing."

"You didn't kill him, hoping we would finish the project and come up with the wrong answer?" Milo winced, thinking how close he had come to doing just that.

"Shoot, I didn't care. I just wanted the big man's name on the report, no matter what he had to say on the subject."

"And nobody else knew you weren't Indian?"

"Nary a one."

"Suppose somebody figured it out, though?" said Milo slowly. "If somebody knew the truth, and didn't realize the politics involved, they might think it was a secret that had to be protected."

"Who would know?" asked Jake.

"Somebody old, maybe, who would remember the truth from childhood."

Comfrey shook his head. "Nope. My mama is the

oldest one, and she's always sworn we come from the Unaka tribe."

Jake looked stricken. "Unaka! No wonder Elizabeth looked funny! I was telling her today that it's the Cherokee word for white man."

"And if she heard it from Amelanchier, she'd wonder what was going on. And she might have gone up to ask her! Does your mother know about this political scheme of yours?"

"No," stammered Comfrey. "She's just an old lady now, and I didn't want to worry her—"

"I think she already knows," said Milo grimly. "Let's go!"

As they hurried out of the church, Dummyweed pulled at Comfrey's sleeve. "Mr. Stecoah, since you guys aren't Indians anyway, do you think I could join the tribe?" He thought it would be very good for the tourist trade.

CHAPTER SEVENTEEN

MILO HAD RUN a hundred yards up the path before he realized that he was staking all his troops on one hunch. Suppose that Elizabeth had not gone to Amelanchier's cabin? He could not afford to be wrong. He also realized that sending four men to confront a woman in her eighties was an embarrassing form of overkill. He motioned for the others to stop.

"What's wrong?" demanded Jake, over the sound of Dummyweed's gasping.

"I think we should split up, in case she went somewhere else. Why don't you and Coltsfoot check the site?"

"Why should she go there?"

"I don't know. To look for more evidence around the graves, maybe. Anyway, we ought to check it out."

"What about you?" asked Jake, cutting his eyes toward Comfrey.

"I'll risk it," said Milo, catching his meaning. "If you don't find her, come up to the cabin."

As they drew nearer to the mountain clearing, Comfrey caught up with Milo and signaled for him to walk quietly. They went the next hundred yards in silence, easing from one point of cover to the next. Milo noticed that Comfrey had not brought his rifle.

"Why are we hiding?" he whispered. "Do you think she'd shoot us?"

Comfrey shrugged. "She's an old woman. If she's protecting our people, ain't none of us safe up here."

Milo was shocked. "But you're her son!" he protested. "Couldn't you pretend you're up here on a friendly visit?"

"I don't know how well she sees at this distance these days, and I ain't about to bet my life that she'd recognize me. Especially if she's already het up over something. I'll do this my way, if it's all the same to you."

When they reached the sourwood tree at the edge of the clearing, Comfrey stopped, studying the cabin. "You wait here and watch me. If I get to the porch okay, I'll give you a signal and you get up there as quick as you can."

Milo tried again. "She's a little old lady," he said, feeling foolish. "Aren't we overdoing this?"

Comfrey looked at him with a troubled expression that means that a mountain person is about to say straight out something difficult for him to express. He decided against it, though, grinned and answered: "Boy, you remind me of the fellow who mistook a coral snake for a scarlet king and died a wiser man. Now stay here and keep your head down!"

As he watched Comfrey creep through the fescue grass, Milo tried to view the whole thing as a scene from a war movie. He knew that if he let his mind dwell on Elizabeth, or on the possibility that they were too late, his reactions would be thrown off, which might undo any chance they had to save her. As if in slow motion, Comfrey passed the woodpile and the dogwood tree, until at last he reached the porch, mounting it not by the front steps, but by a practiced roll around one of the support posts. Milo, who expected to see him ease toward the window, was surprised to see him crawl toward the wooden door instead.

This guy really is a pro, he thought, when he realized how much safer it was to listen than to look. A moment later Comfrey gave him an okay sign of circled thumb and forefinger, motioning him forward.

"She's alive," thought Milo, darting from cover.

His next conscious moment was hitting the porch at a running jump while Comfrey kicked open the door to the cabin.

Milo saw the cramped room, its hand-hewn furniture wedged between cardboard boxes of letters from tourists and piles of packaged herbs. At a plank table in the middle of it all sat Elizabeth, sipping tea from an earthenware mug. When she saw Milo panting in the doorway, she raised her eyebrows, inquiring sweetly: "Return of the ogre?"

"Are you all right?" Milo blurted out before he realized that she obviously was.

"Certainly," Elizabeth informed him. "Amelanchier and I were just talking about ... herbs."

Milo looked at the old woman, whose initial look of surprise had subsided into wariness. "How do, Comfrey," she said crisply.

"We got to talk, Mom," he muttered.

"I reckon you should have thought of that some time back," his mother remarked. "Bit late in the day for it now."

Elizabeth set down her mug, sloshing a bit of tea on the table. "By the way, Milo, you were right about the measurements. I did them wrong."

Milo glanced uneasily at Amelanchier. He didn't see a weapon, but anything could be concealed in the clutter of the room. "We'll talk about that later. You have to leave now."

"What's your hurry?" asked Amelanchier genially. "Stay to tea?"

"What?" asked Elizabeth. She kept shaking her head as if she were drowsy. "Why do I have to leave now, Bill?"

Comfrey glanced at her, then back at his mother. "I believe I'll have a sip of that tea," he remarked.

"I'll fix you a cup, son."

Comfrey picked up Elizabeth's mug. "This'll do me," he said, sipping it.

216

Milo stiffened. "Is it poison?"

"The question is, with what?" grunted Comfrey. "I'd say foxglove, offhand."

Elizabeth laughed, a faraway sound which seemed to echo back through her ears. "Don't be silly! Wise Woman's my friend ... why poison me?"

If there was a reply to this question, Elizabeth did not hear it. She had slumped unconscious to the floor.

Comfrey Stecoah faced his mother with weary resignation. "Mo-*ther!*"

The succeeding hours were much easier on Elizabeth, who slept through them all, than on Milo, who did not. They had wasted precious time explaining the political nuances of the situation to Amelanchier's satisfaction, so that she would tell them which poison had been placed in Elizabeth's drink. That being accomplished, she had thrown in at no extra charge her opinion that they had about half an hour to get Elizabeth to a hospital if they reckoned to save her. It had taken thirty-eight minutes to get her there, even with Comfrey taking the winding roads at speeds Milo seldom tried on straightaways. After the breakneck speed of the first thirty-eight minutes, time slowed down for Milo into a malicious compensation of relative motion, in which seconds could be whiled away like afternoons, and minutes were enough time to read innumerable back issues of *National Geographic*. He waited; filled out forms for the gorgon at the front desk; called Bill; waited; drank seven cups of coffee; waited; talked to Pilot Barnes; waited. At last, someone wearing hospital greens and an expression of authority appeared in the waiting room and said that Elizabeth was sleeping, that her vital signs were stable, that she had come through the treatment as one would expect someone her age to. Milo waited for him to say flatly that she was going to live, but that, it seemed, was not done. "We'll be able to tell for sure tomorrow," was the best answer he could get. Milo wouldn't leave. Jake appeared with a couple of hamburgers, which Milo may or may not have eaten. He didn't know. He was glad to be able to sit there all night, awake, as if by doing so he was earning her recovery. And, if the worst should happen and she did not recover, at least he would be spared the guilt he had felt over Alex, the feeling of not having *tried* to make him live. Of course, he knew how silly he would feel about all of it later.

Two days later, Elizabeth, almost as pale as the pillow propping her up, frowned at the sheet of notebook paper in front of her.

Dear Bill,
I am in the hospital now, having been poisoned by a mass murderer. If you can manage to keep this fact from Mom and Dad, I will be grateful.
I should be out of here in a day or two, and I will come to stay with you then. I don't think I will be *quite* sick enough to go home to Mother, who would probably sign up for a practical nursing course on the strength of this. I promise not to be too much trouble to you; however, the doctors say that on no account am I to do dishes, laundry, or housework of any kind . . .

Smiling at her ingenuity, she paused to await further inspiration.
From just outside the door, she heard a voice say, "Yes, she's awake. I expect she'll be glad to see you."
Elizabeth stuffed the unfinished letter under her pillow and slid down into the proper attitude of

218

convalescence. Through half-lowered eyelids, she watched Milo creep into the room.

"How are you?" he asked, taking the chair next to the bed.

"I tire easily," she said faintly. She turned to give him a limpid gaze, and her eyes widened. "Oh, hell," she said, sitting up. "You look worse than I do."

"You've had more sleep," he said, trying to smile. "Are you really okay?"

"I'm starving." She nodded toward the clean plate on her breakfast tray. "Other than that, fine. But promise you won't tell Bill."

"He's on his way up."

With a sigh, Elizabeth pulled out the sheet of notepaper and tossed it into the wastebasket. "Well, he's too late," she declared. "I solved this murder myself!"

"Yeah, you did. I wish you had told me, though, instead of going off on your own."

Elizabeth raised an eyebrow. "Do you? I thought you didn't want to hear anybody's problems."

Milo reddened. "I don't understand *live* people."

"Yes, and aren't you proud of it! If you'd spend half the time making an effort to understand them, instead of bragging that you can't, you'd be better off!"

"Yeah . . . well . . . I'll try."

"Good. You might start by remembering that live people have feelings. If you hadn't been so sure I was screwing up your precious data, maybe I could have talked to you."

"Yeah. That's what Jake said. He said to tell you he'll be in to see you later. He and Mary Clare are clearing up at the church."

"Mary Clare is back?"

"Yes. She came back yesterday, and if you had waited—" He decided not to start *that* again. "Anyway, those papers she unearthed confirmed our findings about the Cullowhees. It seems that some judge's daughter who was into local color inter-

219

viewed one of them in the 1870s, and she got the whole story."

"So they won't get the land," said Elizabeth sadly.

"Well, actually, it seems they will." He explained Comfrey Stecoah's politics. "He just got a letter from the Bureau of Indian Affairs, and they've scheduled a hearing to discuss tribal status."

"Does the bureau know the truth about them?"

"Not yet. But I think Comfrey is right about their reaction. This morning the *Asheville Citizen* ran a story about Amelanchier being charged with murder, and in the middle of the story they explained about the Cullowhees' not being Indians." He paused for effect. "The headline read: *Indian Healer Charged with Murder*. Of course, most people will remember the headline and forget the truth buried in paragraph five."

Elizabeth sighed. "So they'd have gotten the land anyway. Amelanchier didn't have to protect the secret. She's going to prison for nothing!"

"Don't count on it!" said Milo bitterly. He would never forgive the old woman for the murder of Alex. "She spent about twelve hours in jail, and I'd be surprised if she ever saw the inside of one again. By eight yesterday morning some hot-shot lawyer from Atlanta was up here taking her case for free. He specializes in minority rights. Also in movie rights, from what I hear."

"Well, she is an old woman," Elizabeth pointed out. "You couldn't put her in the penitentiary. Is there going to be a trial?"

"Oh, sure! Everybody is looking forward to that. Half the Cherokee Wigwam Motel is already booked up to newsmen. They're comparing this to the trial of Geronimo." He shook his head sadly. "I'll tell you who *is* going to jail, though. Bevel Harkness."

"Really? Is he the one who broke your computer?"

"Yes—and he swears Amelanchier put him up to it, too. She must have tried that before resorting to murder. But that's the least of Harkness' problems. I doubt if he'll even be tried for it."

"Why not?"

"Because when Pilot Barnes went out to arrest him for breaking and entering, the strip-mining company was out there on the Harkness farm. They were scheduled to do a test strip on his land."

"That isn't illegal, is it?"

Milo shrugged. "It's not what they arrested him for. You see, while he was arguing with Pilot over being arrested, the bulldozer turned up a skeleton."

Elizabeth's eyes widened. "The ringer?"

"Pilot says there was a deputy's badge alongside it. He came to the hospital yesterday and asked me to help Dr. Putnam with a positive I.D. We still have to check dental records, but we're already sure it's the sheriff's nephew."

"It seems I missed most of the excitement while I was camping at death's door," said Elizabeth dryly.

"You provided a lot of it, too," Milo told her. "We were pretty worried about you."

"Good."

"How did you like the dig?" asked Milo hesitantly. "I mean, aside from the...ah...unusual circumstances?"

"I think I'd like to try again," said Elizabeth softly.

Milo understood her to mean more than her choice of careers, but he decided not to press his luck just then. Before he could phrase another question on the subject, the nurse appeared in the doorway carrying an arrangement of flowers.

Elizabeth looked questioningly at Milo, who coughed and said: "Jake is bringing one from me."

"It isn't from Bill," she said thoughtfully, taking the envelope out. "I know him better than that."

Elizabeth took out the card, read it, and looked up at Milo with a puzzled frown. "Milo, who is Duncan Johnson?"

CHARLOTTE MACLEOD

"Suspense reigns supreme" <u>Booklist</u>

THE BILBAO LOOKING GLASS   67454-8/$2.95 US/$3.50 CAN

Sleuth Sarah Kelling and her friend, art detective Max Bittersohn are on vacation at her family estate on the Massachusetts coast, when a nasty string of robberies, arson and murders send Sarah off on the trail of a mystery with danger a little to close for comfort.

WRACK AND RUNE   61911-3/$2.95 US/$3.50 CAN

When a hired hand "accidentally" dies by quicklime, the local townsfolk blame an allegedly cursed Viking runestone. But when Professor Peter Shandy is called to the scene, he's sure it's murder. His list of suspects—all with possible motives—includes a sharp-eyed antique dealer, a disreputable realtor, and a gaggle of kin thirsty for the farm's sale!

SOMETHING THE CAT DRAGGED IN   69096-9/$3.25

The Balaclavian Society only recruited the town's snobs, but was something rotten in the upper crust? Professor Peter Shandy suspects that someone has stooped low enough to murder. And with the help of Police Chief Fred Ottermole and Edmund, Betsy Lomax's feckless feline, he's out to collect the clues that will catch a killer.

Also by Charlotte MacLeod:

THE PALACE GUARD	59857-4/$2.95 US/$3.50 CAN
THE WITHDRAWING ROOM	56473-4/$2.95 US/$3.75 CAN
LUCK RUNS OUT	54171-8/$2.95 US/$3.50 CAN
THE FAMILY VAULT	49080-3/$2.95
REST YOU MERRY	47530-8/$2.95 US/$3.95 CAN

AVON PAPERBACKS

Buy these books at your local bookstore or use this coupon for ordering:

Avon Books, Dept BP, Box 767, Rte 2, Dresden, TN 38225
Please send me the book(s) I have checked above. I am enclosing $_____
(please add $1.00 to cover postage and handling for each book ordered to a maximum of three dollars). *Send check or money order—no cash or C.O.D.'s please. Prices and numbers are subject to change without notice. Please allow six to eight weeks for delivery.*

Name _____

Address _____

City _____ State/Zip _____

MacLeod 6/85

THE MURDER OF SHERLOCK HOLMES
by James Anderson
89702-4/$2.95 US /$3.75 Can

Now a CBS-TV mystery series, MURDER SHE WROTE
starring Angela Lansbury as Jessica Fletcher,
a mystery writer turned detective.

Writing mysteries is Jessica Fletcher's profession,
solving real ones her passion. And when her debonair
publisher invites her to a costume party at his
posh country estate, the guests come as their
favorite fictional characters…and murder shows up
in the guise of Sherlock Holmes!

Also by James Anderson

THE AFFAIR OF THE BLOOD-STAINED EGG COSY
01919-1/$2.95 US /$3.75 Can
A classic 1930's whodunit right up until
the moment the suspects (and that's nearly everyone)
assemble in the drawing room.

THE AFFAIR OF THE MUTILATED MINK COAT
78964-7/$2.95 US /$3.75 Can
A star-struck English Lord, a Hollywood producer,
a hot-tempered femme fatale, a butler named
Merryweather and a whole cast of zany characters in a
particularly pleasing puzzler of mistaken identity,
a mutilated mink coat…
and murder.

AV⊙N Paperbacks

Buy these books at your local bookstore or use this coupon for ordering:

CAN—Avon Books of Canada, 210-2061 McCowan Rd., Scarborough, Ont. M1S 3Y6

US—Avon Books, Dept BP, Box 767, Rte 2, Dresden, TN 38225

Please send me the book(s) I have checked above. I am enclosing $_____
(please add $1.00 to cover postage and handling for each book ordered to a maximum of
three dollars). Send check or money order—no cash or C.O.D.'s please. Prices and numbers are subject to change without notice. Please allow six to eight weeks for delivery.

Name _____

Address _____

City _____ State/Zip _____

ANDERSON 7-85